RESTLESS INK

A MONTGOMERY INK: COLORADO SPRINGS NOVEL

CARRIE ANN RYAN

Restless Ink
A Montgomery Ink: Colorado Springs Novel
By: Carrie Ann Ryan
© 2018 Carrie Ann Ryan
ISBN: 978-1-943123-90-2
Cover Art by Charity Hendry
Photograph ©2016 Jenn LeBlanc / Illustrated Romance

For more information, please join Carrie Ann Ryan's MAILING LIST. To interact with Carrie Ann Ryan, you can join her FAN CLUB

passionate happily-ever-afters." – *New York Times* Bestselling Author Vivian Arend

"Carrie Ann's books are sexy with characters you can't help but love from page one. They are heat and heart blended to perfection." *New York Times* Bestselling Author Jayne Rylon

Carrie Ann Ryan's books are wickedly funny and deliciously hot, with plenty of twists to keep you guessing. They'll keep you up all night!" USA Today Bestselling Author Cari Quinn

"Once again, Carrie Ann Ryan knocks the Dante's Circle series out of the park. The queen of hot, sexy, enthralling paranormal romance, Carrie Ann is an author not to miss!" *New York Times* bestselling Author Marie Harte

DEDICATION

To Mom.
Treasure every moment.
TEM.

RESTLESS INK

The Montgomery Ink series continues with the so-called sensible sister and the one man she never should have fallen for.

For Thea Montgomery, baking isn't only therapeutic, it's also her dream job. She's worked countless hours keeping her bakery afloat, and now that it's where she wants it to be, she's ready to expand and take the next step. When it comes to work and her family, she's on top of her game. Her personal life, however, is a different story.

When Dimitri Carr isn't teaching and hiding his ink under long sleeves to keep the bosses happy, he's trying to be the best brother and friend he can be. After his divorce, he'd thought he would lose Thea from his life forever because she's his ex-wife's best friend. But now that he's free, and the two of them realize they want to keep their friendship. Then he finally sees what he's been missing all this time.

But there are more problems than the fact that Dimitri is Thea's best friend's ex. And when accidental touches and flirtations aren't enough for either of them, and they're finally ready to take the next step, they'll find out exactly what that cost is for crossing that line. And will need to find the strength to face it.

CHAPTER 1

*T*hea Montgomery flopped down on the bed and knew that tonight was the first and last time she'd sleep with Roger. She never should have slept with a man name *Roger* anyway. He was just as dull as his name suggested. She'd gone into date number six thinking that maybe he wasn't as bad as he seemed and wondering if maybe her standards were set too high. After all, not every Roger could be Roger Federer—the king of Rogers and the court.

She'd liked this Roger, at least she'd assumed she did. She'd thought that if she worked harder, they'd have more than just their small attraction. And because she liked sex, and she thought she liked Roger, she'd slept with him.

He let out a pleased sigh beside her, and she held back a sigh of her own—of a very different kind.

This had been a mistake. But not her first, and probably not her last.

Damn it, Thea, get your act together.

Okay, that wasn't fair. She was the sensible Montgomery. The one that joked about sex with her sisters but rarely had it. She'd been too busy starting her business and far too picky to jump into bed with just anyone. And since it had taken *six* dates with Roger to get to this stage, she figured she really wasn't jumping. It was more like a gentle hop.

But there'd been nothing *hopping* in bed with Roger tonight, and now she hated that she sounded so callous about it. Even to herself. He was sweet. He was nice. And... he had no idea what he was doing with his hands or his tongue. And she had a feeling if she were to tell him something along those lines—even gently—and try to show him what she wanted, he'd be one of those guys that pushed back, blaming it on her.

It had happened once or twice.

Okay, four times, but seriously, some guys needed to watch a little less anal porn and a little more cunnilingus. It wasn't that hard.

Roger turned over at that moment and reached out to pat her stomach. She winced since that wasn't the most romantic thing in the world, but then again, nothing about what had just happened could be classified as romance. Ugh, now she felt bad, but there was nothing she could do with her feelings except feel them. Her family had taught her that.

And she *really* shouldn't be thinking of family lessons while naked in bed with a man she wasn't going to see again.

"So...nice, eh?"

Dear God.

"Sure. It was great." She could hear the false note in her tone, but she wasn't sure he could. She hated herself just a bit that she hadn't had any fun, but she'd thought that maybe if she tried hard enough, things would work out.

Apparently, there just wasn't enough chemistry between them, and she probably should have figured that out *before* she got into bed with him, but she'd thought there'd been enough.

"I have an early day tomorrow, but I'll walk you out."

She barely held back a slow blink. Walk her out? Why didn't she just leave money on the table on her way to the door?

She sat up, using the sheet to cover herself since she didn't really feel like baring herself more than she already had and pasted a smile on her face. She'd wanted to leave anyway, but now she felt as though she *had* to. As if she weren't good enough for him to even want to talk to beyond patting her on the stomach like a dog who'd learned a new trick and wanted some love.

Hell, she needed to get out of there before she got angry and said something she would regret. Because before this moment, Roger had been *nice*. Maybe too nice. Perhaps that niceness had covered up his bad sex and selfish ways.

Now, she *really* needed to get out of there. He sat in bed, looking pleased with himself as she put on her panties while still hiding under the sheet. She slid into her dress, not bothering with her bra since she couldn't do that one-handed.

And even as she clumsily tried to dress behind the sheet, he lay there. Watching her.

Why had she thought he was nice?

Oh, because he had been. But not the kind of nice she needed in her life.

Finally, she dropped the sheet since she now wore her panties and dress. She quickly stuffed her bra into her tiny purse, the straps hanging out, slid her feet into her heels, and wrapped her jacket around herself. She'd dressed up for this date and had thought it might lead to something more.

Boy had she been wrong.

"Don't bother locking the door on your way out. I'll get up and do it soon. Wore me out, you know?" He winked, and Thea knew she needed a shower—and maybe a bath, too.

A hot one that would take off the first layer of her skin because she was *never* going to get the feeling of him off her.

What had she been *thinking*? Roger?

Jesus, she needed to take a hard look at her life and maybe never go on another date with a man because she'd seriously never felt this humiliated. It didn't matter that she'd taken her time, done her research on him, and had wanted to make sure she liked him before she went to bed with him. It hadn't been enough.

Men were slime, and Roger was the slimiest.

"Yeah. Sure. Bye."

"Thanks for tonight, babe. I'll call you."

"Don't bother," she whispered as she walked away, her middle finger in the air. It was possible he couldn't see it, but it was still warranted.

"Don't be that way, babe," he yelled from the bedroom where he still hadn't moved, but she ignored him, closing the front door softly behind her. As much as she wanted to slam it, she wouldn't give him the pleasure of her showing any emotion beyond coldness.

Because she was Thea, the ice bitch who played with icing in her bakery. She knew what her exes had said before, and now Roger would just be another of those who thought her cold or something along those lines.

Whatever, she was done with men.

She got into her car, threw her purse onto the passenger seat, and made her way to the grocery store. She was so freaking mad, she didn't even want to bake. That's when she knew that something was wrong, and if she didn't get some sugar soon, she would break—and that wasn't something Roger deserved. And because she didn't want to do something she loved, she knew she was right at the level where she'd start crying in her car, and she refused to do that.

So, she'd go to the store, pick up some ice cream, then eat the whole pint before she went to bed. Alone. Because, of course, she would be alone. Why wouldn't she be?

"Ugh," Thea whispered to herself, annoyed at her train of thought. She hated self-pity, but being tossed out after a particularly bad bout of sex had kind of sent her over the edge into the land of meh.

As soon as she parked, she leapt from the car, purse in hand, and made her way into the twenty-four-hour market. Hopefully, she'd be in and out quickly, and no one she knew would see her do her version of a sugar-loaded walk of shame.

Of course, that's when her heel broke.

Because...of course, it did.

Nothing good ever came from lack of orgasms.

Fuck this night.

Fuck it hard.

Fuck it harder than she'd been fucked.

Though that wouldn't be hard, because...*Roger*.

She picked up the broken part of her heel and limped her way to the frozen food section. She'd be damned if she left without her sugar. Now, though, she'd buy five pints because it was just that kind of night.

Thea was just deciding between the low-calorie fake ice cream and the good old-fashioned heavy cream version when a familiar voice called her name.

"Thea?"

Why *not* tonight? Seriously. Why *wouldn't* this man be right by her after everything that had happened already? Seemed about right.

She rolled her shoulders back and turned to Dimitri, her best friend's ex-husband and Thea's friend, as well. If she were going to meet *anyone* in a grocery store after what had turned out to be a horrible date while wearing a broken heel, her version of the walk of shame outfit, and messy bedhead hair that tumbled down her shoulders in dark waves, it might as well be him.

"Hey, Dimitri."

Dimitri. The man had once been in her life just as much as Molly had. Thea had been friends with both of them and had even known the two separately before they started dating. She'd also refused to take sides during the separation and then after the divorce. Of course, it had always been Molly who wanted Thea to take a side. Dimitri stayed quiet, clearly hurting from the breakup at the time and the changes in his life. He'd tried to keep his friendship with Thea soon after the papers had been signed and even a few months following that, but Thea had always felt awkward because of Molly. Now, she had a feeling she'd made the wrong choice because Dimitri was her friend too, and she'd lost him.

She looked over the line of his jaw, the bend on his nose from where he'd broken it in a bar fight in college—a scuffle that had been about protecting a friend and not because of too many drinks. He wore a cotton shirt under his leather jacket that clung to his wide chest, and jeans that molded to his thighs—not that she was looking at his legs. She knew he had a large tattoo on one quad that was part of his family history, words in Cyrillic that she'd never been able to decipher. He also had a grouping of trees on his forearm and wrist that made a half-sleeve that he'd said reminded him of his family's home. He was a fourth-generation American and had never been to the place his family hailed from, even his last name wasn't Russian, but he'd always loved his ink.

That much Thea remembered about him, even though she hadn't set eyes on him in a month—though it felt like far longer.

His brow rose as he studied her, his gaze traveling down her dress to her broken heel. It wasn't like she could hide anything.

"Are you okay?" He didn't smile as he said it. In fact, he looked angry, really angry. "Do you want me to take you somewhere? To talk?"

She blinked, confused. "What are you talking about? I'm fine." Well, she *would* be fine once she had her ice cream and a long bath, but she didn't need to tell him the details.

Dimitri moved closer and lowered his head so he could whisper in her ear. She ignored the heat of his breath on her neck. Apparently, she was having an off night if she were even thinking about that at all.

"Your dress is on inside out underneath your coat, you have a broken heel, your hair looks tangled, and your bra is in your purse. Are you sure you're okay? Did someone attack you? I'll take you out of here right now and do whatever you need. Just let me help."

Dear. God.

There had to be a better word than mortification for what slid through her right then. If there were a hole opening up anywhere around her, she'd freely jump into it. She'd forgotten about her damn bra and could now clearly remember the straps dangling from her purse. And because she'd been trying to keep the sheet over herself, she'd put on her dress incorrectly, and hadn't noticed because she just wanted out of Roger's place.

Could this night get any worse?

She shouldn't even tempt the fates with that question. She just hoped they hadn't heard her think it.

She wrapped her jacket tighter around her body, willing herself not to cry from sheer mortification.

Thea closed her eyes and took a deep breath. "I'm fine, Dimitri. Embarrassed as hell, but I'm okay." She cleared her throat. "I was on a date."

Dimitri leaned back, eyes wide for an instant before he smiled. "Okay, then."

"Not really okay since he was an asshole and I regret it, hence the ice cream. But I'll be fine. He didn't hurt me or anything. Just bruised my pride."

"I can still beat him up for your pride."

She rolled her eyes. "I'm sure Shep would do that for me, too."

"You tell your brother about your sex life?"

Thea winced and looked over her shoulder to see if anyone was around to overhear. Thankfully, at this time of night, they were alone. That was when she noticed the basket by Dimitri's side full of meats and veggies. Not the typical bachelor fare since she knew he liked to cook and eat healthily. And considering the way he looked, that food did him well.

Okay, enough of that.

"That's just wrong, but on that note, I'm going to get my

ice cream, the full-fat kind because fuck this night, and head home. Thanks for checking on me, though, Dimitri. It was sweet."

"Sweet." Dimitri shook his head. "Thanks for that. You know guys hate that word."

"Some guys do, but you don't because you're not a misogynist prick like some men who won't be named. Anyway, 'night, Dimitri."

He gave her a look, but she waved like a lunatic and grabbed the first two pints of ice cream she saw once she opened the door. Thankfully, both had chocolate in them, so she was good. She left him standing there and felt a little bad about it, but things were awkward between them now thanks to Molly, and Thea was already feeling weird as hell with the whole dress, bra, and shoe thing.

As she limped to the self-checkout—since she'd be damned if she let some night clerk get a good look at her outfit—she prayed that no one else she knew walked into the store. It was enough that she apparently looked as if she'd been assaulted. Though it was nice to know there were good people out there like Dimitri, who actually cared enough to ask if she was okay.

That had to count for something.

By the time she had her ice cream in a bag, and she was limping out the sliding glass doors, her body hurt from walking in a broken heel, and she just wanted to get home. But, apparently, the fates *had* heard her thoughts earlier, because when she got to her car, she let out a watery curse.

"Fuck this," she whispered. "Fuck all of this."

The front driver's side tire was completely flat, and since she didn't see any obvious slashes or holes, that meant it had to be a slow leak. She was exhausted, her ice cream was melting even though it was fucking cold outside, and all she wanted to do was go home. But, apparently, that wasn't going to happen.

She had two options: change it herself since she knew how to do it and had before, or call her brother-in-law, Carter to come and help. He was a mechanic, and since he'd married her sister, Roxie, he had basically put himself on call for any Montgomery vehicle needs. She really didn't want to bother him, though, since he and Roxie were working so many hours these days, so that meant, broken heel and all, she was going to have to change her damn tire herself.

This fucking night.

With a sigh, she opened her car door, tossed her purse and ice cream onto the passenger seat, and went to the trunk to open the back so she could get the spare and everything she'd need to change the tire. It wasn't going to be easy in her dress, but she'd get it done.

"Tonight is just not your night, is it?"

She whirled around, tire iron in hand, then let out a shaky breath when she realized it was Dimitri standing behind her. She hadn't even realized he was parked two spaces away since she hadn't been looking for his car.

"You scared the crap out of me." She put her hand to her chest and slowly lowered the tire iron.

"Shit, I'm sorry, I didn't mean to. But I'm glad you were

ready to hit me if I wasn't me since you're alone out here at this time of night."

She sighed. "It's not that late, and I can take care of myself." Of course, now that she was thinking about it, she'd left the front door of the vehicle unlocked and had her purse visible, so she wasn't making the wisest choices.

"Let me help," Dimitri said quickly. "I'll put these bags in my car and help you with your tire. It's not going to be easy with a broken shoe and in a dress."

She shook her head. "You have perishables. I can handle it."

"I'm sure you can, but you can also let me help. It's supposed to snow tonight so getting home would be a good thing."

She sighed. "I haven't checked the weather since this morning. Snow again?"

"It's Colorado Springs, of course there's a chance of snow at random times even if they didn't mention it twelve hours ago. Seriously, Thea. Let me help, and then you can get home safely and out of that dress."

He cleared his throat after he said that, and it was all she could do not to roll her eyes. It was either that or pant at the thought of taking off her dress in front of him.

Whoa, Nelly.

Where the hell had those thoughts come from? She didn't need to think of Dimitri like that. He was her friend. Kind of. But, seriously, just friends.

"I'd appreciate the help," she said after a moment because, honestly, it was silly to do it all herself when she was wearing what she was, and there was someone who could assist. "But don't make me wait to the side or something. I'll actually help."

"You got it."

He rushed off to his car, practically threw his bags into the back of the SUV, then headed back toward her in less time than it took for her to move things out of the way to reach for the tire.

"Let's see what we can do." He helped her get the spare out of the back, then the two of them got to work. Dimitri did most of the heavy lifting since it wasn't easy in her dress and, frankly, he was stronger than she was. Thea didn't want to stand in his way and make things take more time as the temperature dropped either.

When he bent over, her gaze dropped to his very sexy butt, and she pulled her eyes away. Jesus, what was wrong with her? This was her best friend's ex. There were *rules*.

Rules that kept her away from a very sexy butt and an impressive set of forearms.

No, she was not looking at his forearms. Or his ink. Or the way he held that long piece of metal. Nope.

Why is that tire iron so sexy? Why did she think it phallic?

She'd just seen a penis. It wasn't a nice one, but she'd seen it. She knew what one looked like.

Why was she thinking of Dimitri's penis?

Oh, God, she should have just baked a cake. Or cookies. Or anything that would have kept her out of the damn store.

"All done."

And then he turned and winked, and she knew she was going to hell. A special hell, with only gluten-free products, spoiled eggs, and no yeast.

"Thank you so much," she said, hoping her voice wasn't hoarse because her mind was in a weird place. Namely, the gutter.

"Let me help you clean up." He went to do as he said before she could even answer, so she bent over and picked up a few random things to help out.

When he was done, he gave her a look, then hugged her close before laying a soft kiss on her temple. They both froze.

She couldn't think.

Couldn't breathe.

She took an awkward step back, and he cleared his throat.

"Uh, thanks for your help." She didn't know what else to say. What else *was* there to say?

He let out a breath. "It was good to see you." He paused. "I've missed you, you know. I know Molly said we could still be friends, you and me. But we didn't do that. I showed up a few times to hang out with you, but you always kept me at arm's-length. I thought we were friends and could be in the same room. I didn't—still don't—think there was anything wrong with us being friends. You were my friend before, and I'd like to try that again. So, why don't we?"

She was quiet for so long, she was afraid he'd just leave without waiting for an answer.

"Dimitri..."

He held up his hand. "No, don't say anything. Just think about it. I'll be in touch. Because, Thea? I miss you."

And with that, he walked away, but also kept an eye on her as she got into her car. She knew he was keeping her safe, and she was grateful for that, even as it confused her.

Why *didn't* they try?

The memory of the brush of his lips along her skin filled her mind, and she swallowed hard.

Oh, yeah, that's why.

CHAPTER 2

*D*imitri Carr tugged on his sleeve for the fortieth time that day and held back a sigh. He loved his job, he really did, but ever since he'd moved to this new school district, he'd needed to change a few things about himself that he didn't particularly want to change.

In the two other school districts he'd worked for over the course of his career as a high school math teacher, he'd been able to show his ink while on school grounds. However, with his new superintendent and this new school, he had to hide his tattoos during the day. Most of his ink was under his clothes anyway but hiding a full lower arm piece wasn't easy. And, sure, it was winter now, and he'd be wearing long sleeves at any rate, but the inside of Colorado's schools only had two temperatures.

Blazing hot thanks to the heaters during the winter and part of the early spring.

And freezing cold during the summer and early fall thanks to the air conditioners.

That meant Dimitri sweated during the day since he couldn't roll up his sleeves, but he'd learned to deal, mostly by grumbling to himself when no one was listening.

"Bye, Mr. Carr," one of his senior students called out from the doorway as she waved, passing him on her way to the student parking lot.

"Have a good day, Karin." He waved back and returned to packing up for the day. He had papers to grade at home, but since it was Friday, he had the whole weekend to get it done. He'd probably finish it up tonight, though, honestly, so he could go on a hike and then head to his brother's house for the game. The idea that he was going to spend a Friday night grading instead of out with friends or having some kind of social life was just sad.

As he was packing up the last of his things, his phone buzzed, and he bent to read the screen. Since it was after school hours, he was allowed to have his phone out. One school he'd been at had forced them to constantly be on their phones for a group chat about their teams and other status reports. It had been extreme to the point of ridiculousness, and he was glad to be rid of it.

Though now that he caught the name on his screen, he kind of wished he didn't have to answer. But he reminded himself that he'd made a promise to try and be civil and not ignore her, no matter how many times he wanted to just hit end on the phone and forget that part of his past existed.

But there was a major part of his life still at his old house, so he couldn't do that no matter what he wanted.

He held back his sigh and answered the phone. "Hey, Molly."

Molly. His ex-wife. The woman he'd thought he would one day grow old with. Only, he'd been wrong. They weren't meant for each other. He'd thought they loved each other the right way, but in the end, it wasn't enough. He hadn't been enough for her, and she hadn't been what he needed.

He'd failed at marriage, failed at trying, and every time she called, it was a reminder that he hadn't been able to hack it being the husband she needed.

But he still had to answer the phone every time. Not because of her, but because of who she still had.

"Dimitri, I'm glad you answered. Can you come home?"

It wasn't his home anymore. She'd gotten the house, the home they'd made together, in the divorce, and he'd been left living in a two-bedroom apartment with too-high rent thanks to the housing boom in Colorado Springs. He'd been lucky to even find the place he had, since renting anything these days in this city was a feat of endurance and luck.

Since he'd apparently been silent for too long, Molly continued.

"It's Captain. He's been whining for a walk, but when I go to put him on his lead, he gets all swirly. Can you come and walk him? I have a meeting to prepare for anyway, and it would be better if you just do it. Please? He loves you and misses his Fury."

"I'm on my way."

"Oh, thank you. I could use some help with the bathroom faucet, too. I think it needs a new ring thingy, and I've never been good at any of that. I can learn, but since you already know..."

"I don't know if I'll be able to fix it tonight without the parts, but I'll take a look and make a list."

"Thanks, Dimitri."

She hung up, and Dimitri pinched the bridge of his nose before gathering his belongings and heading out of the classroom and toward the exit and faculty parking lot. It had always been a joke that he was Director Fury to his golden retriever, Captain. Dimitri had been—and still was—a huge fan of that team and would always be Team Captain, no matter the world the current comic and movie franchise inhabited. The fact that Molly had been okay with the name and had even encouraged it when they first got married and adopted the golden retriever had made him feel as if the two of them had connected. But she'd never watched the movies and never wanted to read a comic with him. He hadn't minded since it was okay that they never shared that particular interest, but it made him wonder why she was calling him Fury now.

Shaking that thought off, he drove toward the house he'd made into a home for ten years before being forced to walk away. The thing was, he was glad Molly had gotten the house since he wouldn't want to live in it now, not with the lasting memories of what they'd shared. He hadn't understood why Molly wanted to stay, and since she had a considerable trust fund he hadn't touched in the divorce or even during their marriage, she could have moved anywhere she wanted. But she'd stayed, and he assumed she had her reasons. It wasn't his job to try and figure those out anymore, and while that made him sad, he knew that he would still try to be civil. Maybe not her friend like she seemed to sometimes want, but friend*ly* could work.

Of course, that just made him think of Thea and the fact that he missed her. The three of them had been friends before he and Molly got married, so it was weird that when he was no longer in Molly's life, he was also no longer in Thea's. And because he couldn't stop thinking about how to change that, he knew he would have to figure that out. Maybe he'd go visit Thea tonight at the bakery since he remembered that she worked most Friday evenings so the other workers could have a good start to their weekends.

He still couldn't get the thought of her in that dress and the way she'd appeared at the grocery store the other night out of his head. He'd sworn she looked as if she'd been hurt, and it had taken everything within him not to throw his jacket over hers and carry her out of the store to somewhere safe. Then he'd been embarrassed as hell when he realized exactly why she looked the way she did, and then a little weirded out that he'd been...happy that she hadn't had a good time.

There was something there, something different about his reaction to her, and he knew he'd have to think about it more in-depth later—just not when he was pulling into Molly's driveway. He rolled his shoulders after he'd turned off the engine and prepared himself. It wasn't that Molly was mean or that she ever did anything wrong. In fact, as far as most divorces went, he figured theirs was pretty amicable. It wasn't as if they hated each other. They just didn't love each other anymore. And every time he saw Molly, it reminded him that he'd failed, and that wasn't something he particularly wanted to remember day in and day out.

But he wanted to see his dog and spend time with him, and if his ex-wife needed help around the house, he'd do that, too. It had been his job to take care of the maintenance of the house when they were together. She'd done other things so he didn't have to. They'd had a partnership, each having their own list of chores and upkeep to take care of. And though Molly was learning a lot of what she needed to do now, sometimes, it was just easier for him to do it.

He knew it might not be the healthiest choice, but hell, it was hard to stop ten years of routine when it came to their house. No, *her* house. He needed to remember that.

And though Dimitri had a key, he still rang the doorbell. It wasn't his place anymore, and Molly needed her space, just like he did at his apartment.

She opened the door with a soft smile, but before she could say anything, Captain bounded through the door and right into Dimitri's crotch.

He winced, and Molly laughed as he went to his knees,

hugging his dog and petting him like he hadn't seen him in weeks rather than the few days it had been. He didn't care that it was cold outside or that the snow from the prior night had already melted so now everything was wet, he just wanted to be near his dog.

"Hey, buddy. You're looking mighty fine today." And that was true. Captain was ten years old and completely white in the face, he napped more than he used to, and had some aches in his joints, but he was still a really healthy dog. And if Dimitri had been able to find a damn apartment that allowed pets, he'd have taken his golden with him in a heartbeat. In fact, Dimitri was *still* looking for another place because as soon as he did, and could have Captain, he'd have his dog back. Molly knew the deal when it came to that, and she had agreed, even though Captain had been her dog, as well. It was just that Captain was more *Dimitri's* dog.

The kid they'd never had.

Not that they'd ever really wanted children together. He was just glad that they hadn't had to deal with that part of the divorce, but Captain was still *his*.

"Well, he seems glad to see you," Molly said with a laugh. "Let me get his lead since, apparently, he's ready for his walk now."

At the word *walk*, Captain pranced in circles a few times before sitting carefully on the porch step and raising his paw for a shake. They'd done two rounds of obedience classes over the years, and Dimitri's brothers and sister had helped along the way also, making sure Captain was as trained as a golden could get. Captain was lovable, adorable, and just plain loyal.

And Dimitri hated the fact that the big lug couldn't sleep next to him every night like they had for the past ten years. If Captain were smaller, Dimitri might have been able to sneak the dog into the complex, but there was just no way with the size of his dog.

"Thanks, Molly," he said when she handed him the lead. "I'll be back soon."

She waved him off. "Take your time. I know you hate not seeing him every day. When you get back, I'll have coffee for you if you want. We should talk anyway." There was something in her tone he couldn't quite catch, but he was too tired to deal with it.

He thought of his plans to go to the bakery later and shook his head. "Maybe another time. I'm just going on a quick walk since it's cold out here, but I'll be back this weekend to take him hiking." He'd just pulled that out of thin air, but now that he thought about it, he knew that's exactly what he wanted to do. Captain circled Dimitri's legs, and he started down the walkway so they could get going.

"No problem. If I'm not here, use the key to get him. I know you don't like using it, and I understand and appreciate that, but I also can't be here all the time for you to pick him up."

He nodded. "No problem." He didn't mind using the key at times like those anyway, not when it came to Captain. With one last wave, he headed down the sidewalk and tried to just enjoy his time with his dog. Later, he'd deal with whatever was wrong with Molly's faucet and the other myriad chores he had on his list, but for now, it was him and Captain.

And later...later, he'd go see the friend he missed.

Later.

CHAPTER 3

*B*y the time Dimitri got Captain back to the house and pulled himself away, over an hour had passed, and his stomach was rumbling. He made his way to the highway and drove a couple of exits down to North Academy, where Colorado Icing was located. Thea's building was the second to last unit in the strip, and a couple of doors down from the tattoo shop her brother and sister co-owned—Montgomery Ink Too.

He hadn't been there for the grand opening, but he planned to stop by soon for some new ink. He'd gone to Thea's sister, Adrienne, in the past at her old place down-town, as well as to Thea's cousin up at the original Mont-gomery Ink in Denver a couple of times, but he was glad there was a place with immense talent in his neighborhood. He wanted to finish his other arm soon, and since he already had to wear sleeves, he might as well have both arms done.

He parked in the lot and looked around. He liked the area and shopped at a couple of the other places in the strip, as well. He really liked Teas'd, the newer tea shop near Montgomery Ink Too. The owner was a sweet woman with a sad smile and sorrowful eyes, but she always picked out the best tea for his mood. He had no idea how she did it, but then again, Thea could do the same with sweets and coffee.

Apparently, he was spoiled when it came to this part of town, but he wouldn't complain. He made his way to the bakery, hoping Thea was actually working. If not, he'd still get something sweet to eat before going home to make dinner. It was Friday, so he might as well splurge on his calories for the week since he hadn't yet.

When he went inside, he grinned. Thea was behind the counter, smiling at something another customer was saying. She had flour on her cheek, and if he didn't know better, he'd have assumed she added it daily as part of her work attire. But since the spot seemed to be in a different place every time he came into the shop, he figured it just showed how into her work she actually was.

The place had been updated and painted a few times since she opened, and he thought the clean lines and almost French feel was perfectly suited to her. She'd finished pastry school in Colorado and had stayed because her family was here, and from what he knew, she loved the area, as well. Considering he'd stayed in the city after college too, he didn't blame her. Nothing beat looking at the mountains to the west and wondering every time if it was a surreal painting and not something nature had created.

Dimitri moved forward and toward the front of the shop where he could order a sweet coffee and probably a brownie. He loved Thea's brownies and usually had to work an extra set or four into his workouts so he could glut himself on them. Of course, he also loved her cookies and cakes and even the biscotti, though he hadn't known why people liked biscotti at all before he tried hers.

The customer in front of him left with a coffee in one hand and a plate of frosted cookies in the other and gave Dimitri a nod before taking his seat. Dimitri knew that Thea usually brought orders directly to the table herself, or had one of her servers do it unless it was something simple like a black coffee and a single pastry item. The place was well run, and he had a feeling Colorado Icing was only the beginning for Thea.

"Hey," he said quietly when her eyes widened at the sight of him.

"Hey." She swallowed hard. "You haven't been into the shop in…well, it's been a while."

He smiled, knowing the awkward feeling between them came from his speech the other night in the parking lot. He missed Thea, damn it. She'd been his friend too, and for all her saying she wouldn't take sides in the divorce, they'd each pulled away from each other for Molly's sake. And now he had a feeling he'd made the wrong choice.

He didn't have many friends, not anymore. Most had been his *and* Molly's, and a lot of them had gone to her. He'd understood since they were in different social and financial circles than he was, and most had been in Molly's crowd long before Dimitri met her. But other than his family, he didn't have as many people in his life as he would like.

And he missed his friend.

"I told you I'd try to be by more. For the cake."

She rolled her eyes. "You sure love your sweets. I have no idea how you stay so built."

She blushed, and Dimitri chuckled before raising his brow.

"You're a baker, and I can say the same about you."

She rolled her eyes. "The skinny baker schtick is freaking annoying. I'm not skinny. I have curves. And I work my ass off to keep them. Plus, you know, there's only so many bites of brownies in my life I can deal with."

He resisted the urge to look down at her ass at the mention of her curves. Thankfully, she was angled away so that he couldn't see, but still.

"Speaking of brownies…"

"I have four kinds left today. We had a fifth, but I underestimated this city's love of marshmallows."

"Marshmallows? I missed marshmallows."

She laughed. "Yeah, about ten minutes ago."

"Damn it, I should have brought Captain with me so I didn't miss it."

Her expression softened at the mention of his golden. "I miss him so much. I don't get to see him nearly as often as I would like."

"Same."

She winced. "I'm sorry. That has to suck."

"Pretty much. But I'm still looking for a place that lets in big dogs."

"I'll keep an eye out, as well. I'm sure one of the Montgomerys will be able to find one for you. We're good at things like that."

"I'd appreciate it."

The light flickered above her, and she let out a curse.

"Need help with that?"

"No, I have it. It's that damn light bulb. I switched it out a month ago, and it's already going out again. Meaning, I need to find an electrician. I can probably call one of my cousins who are the only ones I trust since it's their job and they're the best, but it's still a pain in the ass."

She went about getting him a caramel brownie without him even having to ask since, yes, he'd go for caramel if marshmallow wasn't available. Then she set about working on a vanilla latte for him. Apparently, she knew him better than he remembered.

"How late do you work tonight?" he asked as she handed him his order.

"I close tonight since I didn't open. But not too much longer." Something beeped behind her, and she turned, bent over, and reached to tap something on the counter.

He blinked and did his best not to look at her, not to stare. And that's when he knew he was screwed. Because he hadn't been able to get her out of his head, and she was the one person he shouldn't be looking at.

He wanted her as his friend. Nothing more.

And nothing less.

"I don't close tomorrow, though." He blinked as she turned back to him, biting her lip. "And you were right about the whole being friends things. We were friends before you got married, and I miss you, too." She swallowed hard. "So, anyway, I'm having a family and friends game night at my house. Silly games and lots of snacks and booze because…why not. Do you want to come?"

He let out a breath. "I might have plans with my brother. I have to see what he's thinking for tonight, and then I'll let you know. But, Thea? Thanks for the invite."

She smiled. "I hope you can come, but I understand if you can't. It's at seven at my place. Show up if you can."

And with that, he paid for his snack and headed out of the shop, the image of her very pert backside firmly in his mind. He couldn't help but want to kick himself. That was *not* how to keep being her friend, damn it.

And the sooner he got that through his thick skull, the better. Because Thea Montgomery was only his friend. That was all she'd ever been. He'd never thought about her in any other way before this, and he wouldn't start now.

No matter how hard it was.

CHAPTER 4

*H*ow was half the day gone already? Thea shook her head, that same question running through her mind for the eighth time that day. She had worked that morning before handing over the reins to one of her assistants. It wasn't like she worked twenty-four hours a day every day, but sometimes, it sure felt like it.

Once she'd left her bakery, she went to the store to pick up all the groceries she would need to start making everything for their game night. The others had offered to do some of the cooking and were each bringing a dish, but she was the one doing the heavy-lifting.

When her brother, Shep, and his wife and baby girl moved back to Colorado Springs, she and her siblings had decided to start a game night. They did dinners often with the whole family at her parents' house, but this was more for the Montgomery kids, even if the *kids* were all in their thirties and forties at this point. Okay, Roxy was twenty-eight, but Thea wasn't going to think about the fact that she was getting closer and closer to being old.

She already used enough serum and night cream every night to pray away the wrinkles.

She wrinkled her nose, then stopped, remembering the time her mother had said that wrinkling her nose—or wrinkling anything—would lead to wrinkles in general. She was already thirty years old and counting on upcoming fine lines and the oncoming gray hairs. Maybe if she focused more on her personal life instead of just her work life and business, she wouldn't be looking for every nonexistent wrinkle and gray hair.

And now she was once again thinking herself into a corner, so she pushed those weird thoughts out of her mind and stared at the groceries in front of her on the kitchen counter.

She already had a few things in the oven, chilling in the fridge, and simmering in the crockpot, but she still had a couple of other things to make and bake. She should've just brought some stuff home from the bakery. But in her mind, she wanted to make something special for her siblings. She hadn't wanted to bring work home, but rather make this a family thing. A family and *friends* thing now since, sometimes, Abby, her new friend and fellow business owner, joined them, as did Kaylee, another business owner and artist. Those two weren't coming tonight, but they were planning on coming next time. It wasn't easy to match everybody's schedules, and Thea understood that. And considering that she had invited Dimitri, who she was pretty sure wouldn't be able to come, she really understood that.

Thea still couldn't believe she had invited him. Dimitri and Molly had already been divorced by the time Shep moved up north. That meant they were already having big game nights when he was in her life—at least more than he was now. But they were both trying to change that. It was still awkward, but she was glad that she'd invited him. He had been the one to put himself on the line and ask to be friends again, so she'd decided to take the step she had.

And she was only slightly disappointed that he probably wouldn't be able to make it.

Her stomach rolled, and she frowned. Okay, so maybe she was more than slightly disappointed, but that didn't mean anything. Just because she had watched the way he moved in his jeans, and noticed the way her eyes always glanced at his forearms didn't mean that their friendship was going to be any different than it was. It just meant that she was going to have to split her time between Molly and Dimitri.

And now she felt a little sick, and a little bit like she wasn't making the right choices. She needed to talk to Molly to make sure the other woman was okay with Thea hanging out with Dimitri. Her best friends had said more than once that Thea didn't have to make a choice, didn't have to take sides. But she was going to double-check, just in case. Because the last thing she wanted to do was hurt her friends.

Knowing that she was probably making too much of it, Thea started the call to Molly, putting it on speaker so her hands would be free to continue work around the kitchen. Molly picked up on the third ring, her voice soft and sweet.

"Hey there. I was just thinking about you. I take it you have the afternoon off?"

Molly didn't work a nine-to-five job and usually only volunteered for different committees and charities around the city. More often than not, her friend was up in Denver, working with the bigwigs, trying to raise funds for one cause or another. Molly came from money, and she'd never held a job where she earned a wage for herself. Then again, the amount of time and energy that the other woman put into raising money for others constituted more than a full-time job in Thea's opinion. At least the times when Molly was actually working. Sometimes, Molly got burned-out from volunteering and committees and jumped into the Denver socialite circles. Thea hadn't even known that existed before she and Molly became friends, but then again, that wasn't her world. From what Thea could remember, it wasn't Dimitri's either.

"Thankfully, yes. I didn't know if I was going to actually work today at all, but you know me, I can't stay away."

"You and your baked goods, Thea. Luckily, you don't sample every single piece you make, or your ass would be twice as big."

Thea winced and did her best to try and take that as a compliment. After all, Molly's butt was firm, high, and tight, but she also had far more time to go to the gym and work with her personal trainer to ensure it stayed that way. Thea walked the hills of her neighborhood. She never ran. The idea of running unless there was a serial killer chasing her made her want to throw up. She would just deal with any extra pounds on her behind.

"Thankfully," Thea said dryly. "Anyway, I was calling to see if you wanted to come to game night tonight. I know I've invited you before, but you weren't able to make it. Just letting you know that we'll have an extra seat in the circle if you're interested."

"Oh? Who's coming?"

"The usual. My brother, Shep. His wife, Shea. My sister, Adrienne and her dude, Mace. And my other sister, Roxie, and her husband, Carter." Thea paused, wondering if she should say who else she'd invited, then thought she might as well broach the subject that she'd actually called about. "I also invited Dimitri since he and I are friends, but he doesn't think he'll be able to make it since he might be going to visit his brother. So, you're not going to have to deal with that if that would be an issue. Is it an issue?"

Not the smoothest way to bring it all up. But now, it was out in the open, and she would go with it.

"That sounds like it's going to be fun. I can't make it, but I'm glad you invited Dimitri. He seemed a bit lonely the last time I saw him. Maybe you and your family can cheer him up. Anyway, I must be off, I'm going shopping with the girls to find a new dress for our next event. You have no idea how hard it is to find something these days. Have fun tonight, and give Dimitri my...well, just have fun."

And with that, her friend hung up, and Thea just shook her head, a smile playing on her lips. That might've been a strange conversation, but it was still very much a Molly conversation.

Shaking off that weird feeling, Thea went to make her veggie and cheese plates. She'd only bought three cheeses because Shep had made fun of her last time when she had an array of ten. But she was a cheesemonger and loved all things cheese. She was even an honorary Green Bay Packers fan, merely because of the headwear. She'd been ten when she made that choice, and she still had jerseys and the foam cheesehead that she wore when she was alone in her house watching the games. She figured if she hadn't become a baker, she probably would have become a chef who worked primarily with cheese.

She didn't necessarily think the smellier the better, but she liked smelly, and she liked buttery. For tonight, she'd only bought a Gouda, some cheddar, and a soft white, which pretty much rounded out the main cheese groups. Of course, now that she looked at the plates, she realized that some of her favorites were missing, as well as some of her favored crackers, but she didn't have enough time to head to the grocery store to get more. Plus, she didn't want to deal with her brother making fun of her in her own house, so three cheeses would have to do.

Thea put on her latest audiobook about a fae prince and a human woman and finished getting the food ready, along with setting out a selection of cookies and brownies because there was no way she was hosting a party without baked goods. Once things were either warming, cooling, or setting, she went to work cleaning up around her home, straightening pillows and tossing blankets artfully along the couch like her mother had taught her to do. None of her siblings were particularly amazing when it came to decorating or keeping their houses perfect, but that's not what her parents had taught them. Instead, all of their homes had their own touches with the little bit of mess that came from living.

Thea had bought her house the same year she opened the bakery. She'd been living on ramen and canned green beans along with any stale cookies from her shop for over a year because of it. She hadn't meant to go into that much debt all at once, but her perfect three-bedroom house with its mountain views and a full wall of windows facing that view had gone on sale during the best buyer's market ever. She'd practically bled for the loan paperwork and had almost been forced to ask her parents to co-sign—something they had already offered—but in the end, she had her house and her business.

Just no one to share them with.

She pushed those thoughts out of her mind as she pulled the games out of the closet, setting them on the coffee table. The others would bring their games with them since it never made sense to store all of them at one house since they alternated game nights between each of their homes.

Thea let out a breath and stared at the random assortment of board and drinking card games she had. It was a silly way to spend the night and, honestly, for a bunch of tattooed and pierced people, they were all pretty lame when it came to nights out. But as two of their four had children in their homes and rarely had time off, it just made sense for their nights to age as they did. Of course, they all had guys' nights and girls' nights where copious amounts of drinking occurred, but tonight would be a little tamer.

She thought about the bottles of wine and whiskey she'd already set out and grinned. Okay, so tonight might not be *that* tame in the end, but at least one of each of the couples would stay sober, or they'd do like last time and Lyft it to her house.

Thea smiled then wondered how, once again, she'd ended up the single one at her own party. And while she loved the idea that her siblings were either married or well on their way to being so, she hated the idea that she'd somehow been left behind.

She'd spent so long working on her career and her house, that she'd forgotten human interaction. Images of her night with Roger came back to her, and she gagged. Ugh, maybe human interaction was overrated since she had absolutely no desire to ever get back into bed with Roger or his ilk.

Not that he'd actually called or even texted her since she'd left his house, but still.

Men sucked.

Of course, as soon as she thought that, Dimitri came to mind. Well, *he* didn't suck. He was always nice to her, caring, and helpful. And now it sounded as if she were describing his golden retriever. But that's what came with doing her best *not* to think about his ass, his forearms, or his smile.

Nope, not thinking about those.

Instead, she ran back to her bedroom, touched up her makeup and hair since she'd been working and moving around all day, switched into a long, black, racerback maxi dress and shrug, and walked back out into her living room to make sure everything was going according to plan.

The doorbell rang as she was stirring the meatballs in her crockpot, her mouth watering since she loved them almost as much as she loved cheese and baked goods. She gave them one last stir and went to open the door.

Shep and Shea walked in, giving her tight hugs that she knew she'd never get tired of. Her brother had lived in New Orleans for years after finding a tattoo shop and crew he fit into like another family. He'd even met his wife down in the big easy. Thea had missed him every damn day and had hated the fact that he'd been down there for so long, having a life of his own.

Then, last year, he'd come back with Shea and their daughter Livvy, and Thea barely resisted the urge to tuck them all close and never let them out of her sight. She might not be the oldest sibling—in fact, she was the second youngest—but she sure acted like the eldest most of the time.

"We brought Pictionary," Shea said wryly, her blond hair in ringlets around her face. She looked like an angel in Thea's opinion, but she loved her sister-in-law like she was her true sister. Apparently, Shea's family was horrible beyond measure, but that just meant that Shea was a Montgomery now no matter what. There was no going back—not that anyone wanted her to.

"Wasn't there a flying pen incident last time?" Thea asked, her eyes wide, her mouth twitching as she held back a laugh.

Shep rolled his eyes, his hands full of games and beer. Shea held what looked like bacon tortilla roll-ups and hip-bumped her husband.

"You were the one that threw the pen if I recall," Shea said, fluttering her lashes.

"It was one time, and I don't want to talk about it. Now can I put this down and take off my coat? I'm roasting in here."

Thea just snorted and took the beer from his hands so he could easily handle the other stuff he held. Shea followed Thea to the kitchen where, after Shea took off her jacket and shoes, the two of them started working on setting up the food areas.

When the doorbell rang again, Shep called out, "Got it!"

Thea just shrugged. Her hands were full, and it wasn't like it would be anybody but family anyway.

Adrienne and Mace came in, their hands brimming with more games and a seven-layer dip. Before they could even say hello, Roxie and Carter were behind them, wine in their hands.

"Sorry, we didn't have time to cook," Roxie said apologetically.

"But we brought wine," Carter said, leaning into his wife.

Roxie gave him a sad look over her shoulder that she quickly blinked away, and Thea held back a frown. Her sister and brother-in-law were still newly married and so in love it hurt to see sometimes. But even as she thought that, she knew the two were having problems. What those problems were, Thea didn't know, but she hoped her sister would open up to her soon. Adrienne had mentioned it to Thea, as well as Shea, but the three of them were holding back, hoping the couple could work it out on their own.

And, hopefully, Roxie would understand that they were all there for her if she needed them. Thea didn't know if Shep had noticed yet, but her brother was far more observant than she gave him credit for sometimes.

Whatever the case may be, whatever was happening between Roxie and Carter, was between them, and somehow, the Montgomerys weren't going to interfere.

Thea held back a wince. She knew her family, and knew that wouldn't be the case for long.

Pushing that thought aside, Thea quickly wiped her hands on a kitchen towel and went out to hug the newcomers and make sure everyone had a drink in his or her hand. She was just kissing Mace's bearded cheek when the doorbell rang again.

The rest of them looked at one another, their brows raised.

"I thought Abby and Kaylee couldn't make it," Roxie said.

Thea licked her lips, her stomach rolling as she put a smile on her face. "I, uh, might have invited one more person."

Adrienne's head tilted. "Molly?"

"Not exactly." She turned and opened the door to find Dimitri standing on her doorstep, his hair wild in the wind, his leather jacket perfectly molded to his body, and the smile on his face warming her in places she had no right to feel heat.

Tonight would require a lot of wine.

So much wine.

"Dimitri," she said with a smile. "I didn't think you were going to make it."

"My brother ended up having other plans. I hope it's okay I came." He paused. "I brought cheese."

She looked down at the seven kinds of cheese on his plate and was pretty sure she had a little orgasm.

He'd brought her cheese. All the cheese. She could totally fall in love with this man.

And where was that wine?

"You know me and my cheese. Come in. Everyone just got here, and I'm going to have to try all that cheese. I'm just saying."

Not the greatest of things to say, but she was beyond flustered. She just wanted him inside her house where he'd be comfortable, and she could try to catch her breath. She had no idea why she was reacting this way now when she never had before when he was married to Molly but, apparently, time and distance had given her a whole new outlook on the man—one she wasn't sure she wanted at all.

Her siblings gave her looks behind Dimitri's back, and she just smiled. The man was her friend, nothing more, and that had always been the case. She was just happy that Molly hadn't been able to come, or it would have been awkward. Because even though the two of them saw each other often for Captain's sake, Thea didn't want that energy and situation under her roof.

And that meant no thinking about Dimitri the way her mind kept wanting her to.

Because no matter how many types of cheese he brought to her, she knew he was off-limits, and she and her cheese-loving self, as well as her tingling lady parts, could get the fuck off.

Okay, maybe *back* the fuck off would be a better phrase to use.

Roxie came into the kitchen as Thea unwrapped Dimitri's glorious cheese plate and held out a glass of wine. "Want to talk about it?"

"Talk about what? How I'm going to kick your ass tonight?" Was she talking high and fast? Because she felt like she was talking high and fast.

"No, I was talking about your new teammate."

She frowned. "Teammate? Since when are we playing on teams?"

"Since Adrienne brought it up. There's eight of us now. Shep jumped on the chance since Shea usually kicks his ass on trivia and he wants her on his team. Plus, he probably wants to size up Dimitri."

"Why would he want to do that?"

"Because of the lingering looks you and he gave each

other over his cheese." Roxie smiled, her eyes full of laughter. Thea shushed her.

"Shut up. He'll hear you."

"Meh, he should know what he's getting into when it comes to being with the Montgomerys."

"There's no being, no circling, nothing to keep a watch out for or size up. Now, once again, shut your mouth and go give Dimitri a beer. He likes the amber ale I have in the fridge."

"Of course, you know that."

"Because he was married to my best friend, Roxie."

Her sister gave Thea a sad look then kissed her on the cheek. "Got it. For now. But we're still playing teams, or we'll be here all night playing Pictionary because Shep holds a grudge.

Thea laughed then, wine in one hand, and went to bring out Dimitri's cheese plate—after stuffing a slice of buttery brie into her mouth.

Dimitri tilted his beer toward her. "Thanks. You remembered."

"It's my favorite too, so I had it."

"I know." He smiled. "Now, let's see how the Montgomerys play."

"You're going to regret you said that," Mace said with a laugh.

Carter visibly shuddered before crossing himself.

Thea just grinned. "Game on, partner."

CHAPTER 5

Thea knew she'd had one too many glasses of wine by the time her family walked out of her house to their waiting drivers. All of them had opted to use Lyft rather than drive, and for that, Thea was grateful. Hell, she was glad all she had to do was clean up before going to bed. No one had made too much of a mess, and everyone had helped clean up some of it already, but she just wanted to sleep.

Of course, one person had stayed behind to help her, and now she was *sure* she'd had too much wine. She was tipsy, not drunk, and much too warm to make any good decisions. So, she wouldn't make any.

"You don't have to stay, Dimitri."

"I'm helping you clean. You might be able to push your family out because they're going to host soon, but you can't push me out."

She narrowed her eyes at him. "How drunk are you? Should I be calling you a Lyft, too?"

He shook his head. "I had a few beers and will schedule my own Lyft. I like that we all did that instead of trying to risk it. Makes me happy that you all think ahead."

"We don't drink together that often anymore and, apparently, that final game of Twister sent us all over the edge."

Dimitri snorted. "I still think you cheated on right foot yellow."

She gasped. "Liar. I didn't cheat. You fell. You don't have the moves to twist, Dimitri. Just let it be known."

"Cheat."

Her face warmed, and she went right up to him, tilting her head back since he was so much taller. "What? I could beat you again, and we both know it."

He held up the board and casually flicked the spinner. "Prove it."

"Just the two of us? I don't think so."

"Bawk."

"Did you just...did you just make a chicken noise at me?"

"I'm sorry, I can't hear you, all I hear is clucking. Bawk."

She lifted her chin, then stripped off her shrug so she wore only her maxi dress. She needed space to move, and it wasn't easy to play in a dress to begin with, but she was no cheat. She ignored the way Dimitri's eyes followed her movements, thinking the warmth she felt had to be the wine, nothing else.

"Fine. Game on."

Dimitri just smiled, and soon, the two of them were

standing on the floor mat, laughing like loons as they tried to twist. Having him spin for the two of them wasn't easy, but she'd be damned if she allowed him to call her a cheat.

Only, when she went for left foot green, her leg twisted with Dimitri's and they both went down. He tried to move so he took the brunt of the fall, but her dress got in the way, and she ended up on her back, her dress hiked up to her thighs, and Dimitri nestled between them.

She stiffened, her breath going ragged.

"Shit," Dimitri muttered. "Shit."

She didn't say anything, couldn't say anything. She could only feel him, feel the wine in her system. She wasn't drunk enough to make a mistake, but not sober enough to move away from him either.

And when his breath warmed her cheek, she did the one thing she shouldn't, she tilted her head ever so slightly, so their lips brushed.

And then, she was lost.

CHAPTER 6

*D*imitri knew this was a mistake, knew Thea knew it was a mistake, but he didn't pull his mouth from hers. Instead, he deepened the kiss, taking her mouth with his as her lips parted with a gasp. He rocked against her, knowing he shouldn't, but doing it anyway. When one of her legs lifted a bit higher so her calf rested on the back of his thigh, he held back a groan, angling his mouth more so he could deepen the kiss.

Thea was the one who groaned, and he slid his hand up her side, bracing himself on his forearm so he didn't put his full weight on her. As it was, his too-hard cock pressed firmly against the heat of her. With her dress riding up the way it was, he knew the only thing separating them was the scrap of her panties and his pants.

He kissed her harder, rocking into her as she arched for him, her hands sliding up and down his back with increasingly sure strokes. When he gently bit down on her jaw, she gasped, whispering, "Dimitri," and he knew he had to pull back. He was barely able to catch his breath.

"We need to stop." He swallowed hard, his forehead against hers.

"I know." Her hands didn't stop moving, though. And when her thighs tightened as he rocked again, he kissed her once more, knowing they were making a mistake yet not stopping himself. His head was full of lust and booze, and though neither of them was drunk enough for them to take advantage of one another, they were both tipsy enough to make the wrong choices.

But a choice this seductive wasn't one he could walk away from.

So, he didn't.

Instead, Thea tugged on his shirt. He leaned up so he was kneeling between her legs and pulled his Henley over his head. Then he licked his lips at the sight of her, all curves and sex...and *his*, if only for the moment.

He leaned over her again, sucked on her bottom lip, then reached for her dress. "Off."

She arched her back, giving him the space he needed so he could pull the long dress over her head. Then he just about swallowed his tongue at the sight of her light pink nipples, hard and tight on full breasts that practically begged for his tongue.

"No bra?" he rasped.

"Didn't work with the dress."

"Jesus." Then, he was over her again, his mouth on her

breasts, sucking, licking, cupping. She ran her fingers through his hair, tugging when he bit down on her nipple, flicking his tongue over the rigid tip to soothe the sting. When he lifted his head to blow cool air over the pink point, she shivered, moaned. So he did the same to her other nipple, going slow and steady even though all he wanted was to sink into her.

This is such a damn mistake.

He pushed those thoughts out of his head and kept licking her skin, needing her taste. Wanting more, he moved down her body, leaving bites and kisses along the curves of her stomach and hips, lashing a long lick up the line of her hip bone.

"Di—Dimitri."

"You like?"

"I...I can't think." Then she spread her legs, and he took that as an answer. She wore a black cotton thong that, for some reason, was the sexiest thing he'd ever seen in his life. She was all curves and smooth skin, and he wanted to eat up every inch of her—and, damn it, he just might.

When she placed her leg over his shoulder, he smiled. His Thea wasn't shy, and he was a damned happy man. Then he lowered his head, pressing a kiss over her panties, finding her hot, and the cotton drenched.

So damn sexy.

He pulled her panties to the side, blowing cool air over her pussy, her folds wet and clearly needing his touch. So, Dimitri lowered his head, licking and sucking, flicking her clit with his tongue. She made small whining sounds, and he knew she needed more. So, he leaned up, ignoring her confused glance when he stopped and tugged off her panties. She helped him by moving her legs out of the way, then he went back to eating his woman out.

He ignored the possessive quality of his thoughts, knowing it had to be the booze talking, even if he didn't feel buzzed anymore. At least not on beer.

He sucked and licked, using his fingers to tease her as he tasted her, and when he breathed cool air again, he made her come.

She gasped, arching her back with her hands on her breasts, playing with her nipples as she came.

It was singularly the most stunning image he'd ever seen in his life.

And as she was still shaking in his hold, he gripped her hips and flipped her over onto her stomach.

"Jesus, Dimitri."

"I love your ass. So thick and bitable." He palmed both globes in his hands, molding, spreading her cheeks so he could see all of her.

"A girl doesn't want to hear that her ass is thick," she breathed.

"Your ass is mine tonight, Thea. So let me play."

She looked over her shoulder, her brow raised. "Uh, what do you mean by that?"

He dipped his finger between her crease, grinning as she sucked in a ragged breath. "I'm not going to fuck you here, but I'm going to make you scream my name."

Then he lowered his head and bit her ass, loving the way

she gasped but didn't back away. Instead, she pressed her soft curves into his face as he licked and sucked on her pussy and ass before biting down on her clit. She came again on his face, not bothering to hold it back.

And he relished it.

He wanted to be inside her so damn badly, but he remembered what he was missing.

"Fuck."

"That's the point, right? Get inside me."

He grinned at her sass, slapping her on the ass.

"Hey!"

"I don't have a condom, babe."

She went on all fours and reached for her purse that was on the floor near them. It must have fallen earlier. She dug around then pulled out a condom, a wicked grin on her face.

"Got one."

"Love a woman who's prepared."

"Yeah, yeah. Get those pants off and get in me, Dimitri. Now."

He stood up, shucked off his pants, ripped the condom open, then slid it down his length. He was so damn hard, he was afraid he wouldn't last long, but with the way Thea licked her lips, he wasn't sure she would mind, not with how many times she'd come already.

She wiggled that ass in front of him, and he lowered to his knees, gripping her hips.

"Ready?"

In answer, she slid her wet heat over him.

So he pushed, *hard*.

He was in her in one thrust, both of them gasping at the same time. She was so tight around him, so wet, so hot, that he stopped moving. He froze as he waited for her body to accommodate him. Then he leaned over her, kissed the back of her neck, and she tilted her head slightly so they could look each other in the eyes.

"Move," she whispered.

He took her lips, then he *moved*.

He slid in and out of her, breathing hard as she met him thrust for thrust. When his balls tightened, and his back tingled, he pulled out of her, then flipped her over again. She arched for him as he slid into her again. He needed her mouth as he fucked her, as she fucked him. Then she was suddenly on top of him, riding him with his hands on her breasts and her head thrown back like a goddess.

And when they both came, he was pretty sure he literally saw stars that had nothing to do with a knock on the head.

When Dimitri could think again, he ran his hand down Thea's sweat-slick back, his body still shaking from aftershocks. She stiffened at his touch before levering herself over him, his dick still semi-hard inside her. She didn't bother to cover up her breasts, and he barely resisted the urge to reach out and pluck at her delicate, pink nipples. He'd tasted every inch of her, even in his buzzed haze, but he wasn't feeling the alcohol anymore. In fact, he was pretty sure he'd burned it all out of his system even if he hadn't burned off all the lust.

"Thea."

Gone was the woman who'd flirted back, who'd wiggled her ass on his face as if she couldn't get enough of him. Gone was the woman full of confidence.

Gone was the Thea that had been with Dimitri.

She held up her hand, her face pale, her eyes glassy. Then she slid off him, the action sending shivers down his spine, but he willed himself not to react. This wasn't the time for that, and hell, he didn't know what he wanted anyway. He couldn't believe what had just happened. Couldn't believe they'd done that—too much wine and beer or not.

When she stood up and went to the end table for the tissue box, he reached out for a few from her and cleaned himself off, tightly wrapping up the used condom. Then she wordlessly held out a small wastebasket so he could dispose of the mess. Her face was blank enough that he had no idea what she was thinking, what she wanted him to do beyond the basic mechanics of ridding himself of the condom and the evidence of what they'd just done. She wrapped an afghan around herself, covering herself from his gaze.

And since she still hadn't said anything, he sat up and reached over to pull on his pants as well as the rest of his clothes. He had no idea what he should say, but he knew he needed to say *something*.

"Thea," he said again as he pulled on his shirt.

"No. You need to go. Just…just go."

"We need to talk."

She pressed her lips together in a thin line, but before she could say anything, his phone rang. He cursed since he recognized the ringtone—and so did Thea.

"Answer it," Thea said.

"Thea."

"Answer the phone. Molly might need you for Captain."

He let out another curse and grabbed his phone, even as he winced at Molly's name on the screen—the ghost between them that wasn't so much a ghost now.

"Molly," he said briskly as he answered.

"I need you over here, Dimitri. Captain won't eat, and I'm worried."

His phone must have been loud enough, because Thea seemed to hear the words as well, her face going impossibly paler.

"Go," she mouthed.

"I'll be right there. Try to get him to eat, Molly."

"I've *tried*, Dimitri. It's not working. I need you."

Thea took a step back at those words, and Dimitri felt as if he'd been kicked in the gut.

"Be there soon." He hung up and looked at Thea, still wrapped in her blanket, her hair tousled, her lips kiss-swollen, her lipstick faded and smeared. She looked so fucking beautiful, and he had no idea what to say just then.

"Just go," she said. "Because...well...you just need to."

"We're not through with this."

"We already are."

He let out a breath, rolling his shoulders back. "No, we aren't."

She didn't say anything else, but he wasn't sure there *was* anything to say. He needed to go to his ex-wife's house to take care of his dog. The same ex-wife that stood between him and Thea. He wanted to be Thea's friend, and yet…and yet, that had changed, hadn't it?

He didn't know what he was going to do after he left Thea's place, but he knew he needed to leave, to give her space.

And then, after that? He really didn't know. But when the door closed behind him, he heard her lock the deadbolt into place, and he prayed he hadn't just fucked everything up. He slowly walked to the end of the street and ordered a Lyft to his house so he could get his car. He was sober now, so damn sober that he felt every mistake he'd made by not voicing his thoughts.

He'd fucked up.

And he had no idea how to fix it.

CHAPTER 7

*D*imitri pulled into Molly's driveway and tried not to think about what he'd just done with Thea. He knew that, at some point, Molly might need to know since she was friends with Thea, but it wasn't his place to say anything. Somehow, he'd put Thea in the middle of everything, though he'd done his best not to do so since the divorce.

To say he'd fucked up was an understatement.

He liked Thea, always had, but he'd never looked at her the way he had tonight until recently. She'd always been his friend. *Molly's* friend. Dimitri had loved his wife and had been faithful. He'd never even thought of being with another woman while he was married. And when the divorce came, when he and Molly didn't love each other anymore, he'd tried to figure out what had gone wrong, only to realize there wasn't a clear answer.

Some relationships just didn't work. And he and Molly didn't work at all. Not anymore. And the more he thought about it—something he did more often now that he was alone—he wasn't sure they'd ever fit. He'd loved her with everything he had at the time, but he'd always been on the periphery of her life. The same with her in his. They shared friends, friends that had all gone to Molly after the divorce. They'd shared Captain, but he was really Dimitri's dog— hence why Dimitri was here late at night, about to go into the home he'd once shared with Molly to feed his best friend.

Molly should have called earlier, but it was almost as if she'd known exactly the worst time to call and interrupt. The time that it would have the most detrimental emotional impact on his life—on Thea's life. Of course, his ex hadn't known, and it had just been a horrible set of circumstances, but there was nothing to change that now.

Dimitri had to go inside, get the dog he wanted by his side to eat, and then leave before there were too many questions asked that required answers he honestly didn't have for Molly.

And, frankly, he wasn't sure if it was his ex-wife's business at all what happened between him and Thea. That thought made Dimitri sound like an asshole since common decency dictated he should walk away and not let it happen again and make sure Molly knew, but he wasn't sure he could do that. Not when he *felt* like there might be something between him and Thea. He'd been trying hard to make sure they could remain friends, but apparently some part of him wanted more.

He needed to get home and think on it, try to piece together exactly what he was feeling so he didn't mess up what he already had with Thea—beyond what he'd torn away.

And that meant not telling Molly a single thing until he talked things over with Thea.

This isn't going to be awkward at all.

He ran a hand down his face, aware he hadn't changed or even brushed his teeth after Thea's place, but he hadn't had time. It was late, and his dog needed him. He hoped to hell that he'd be able to find a new place soon with his limited funds because he wanted Captain to live with him. Molly couldn't get him to eat or walk some days, and it was killing Dimitri more each day to witness it. Captain was suffering because Dimitri wasn't there. Enough wallowing. Dimitri needed to get inside, no matter the awkwardness.

He got out of his car and headed to the front door. Molly opened it without him even knocking, as though she were waiting for him. He held back a sigh and raised his chin.

"Where is he?" he asked, his voice a little gruffer than intended. He was tired, off-kilter thanks to Thea, but he knew he shouldn't take it out on Molly. She hadn't done anything wrong, and if anything, she just wanted Captain to be happy and healthy.

He cleared his throat and started again. "Sorry, thanks for calling. Where is he?"

She just shook her head. "Don't be sorry. It's late, and I

hate that I had to call you at all. I thought you'd be in Denver with your brother, actually."

He blinked, not remembering if he'd told her those plans or not. But it had been a long day, so he let that thought slide from his brain. He'd probably mentioned it earlier when he picked up Captain up for their hike. The fact that he'd spent a few hours with Captain today, and the dog still wouldn't eat worried him, so he made a move toward the den.

"I decided to stay in town." To see Thea, but he didn't mention that to Molly.

"Then you made it to game night?"

He stiffened. "Yes, actually." Thea must have invited Molly, as well. After all, they were friends. And...this was getting far too complicated. The smart thing to do would be to stay out of Thea's life, but he honestly didn't know how smart he was anymore when it came to Thea Montgomery.

He purposely let his shoulders relax. "The Montgomerys were there in force. Adrienne and Mace won. They're all very competitive. Not surprisingly."

"So I hear," Molly said, smiling. "They've always been that way for as long as I've known Thea. I might have to join them next time. I had to say no for tonight, but maybe not in the future."

Dimitri just nodded, a weird feeling crawling over him. Guilt. He knew he shouldn't feel it, but he did. This was so damn complicated, so tangled, and he knew that Molly *had* to be told the truth. But not until he talked to Thea. This was Thea's truth to give just as much as his, and they needed to be on the same page about it, or at least know what pages existed before they told Molly anything.

Once again, he was an asshole.

"Anyway, Captain is in the den. I have his food next to him, but I think he's sulking."

Dimitri winced. "Sounds about right. The vet says he's fine."

"Just misses you." Molly's eyes filled with tears, and she blinked them away. "Sorry. I just hate that he's like this."

Dimitri resisted the urge to reach out to hug her and give her comfort. He still smelled of Thea and knew he should have showered, but he'd wanted to get to his dog as soon as possible. In doing so, he'd crossed so many lines it wasn't even funny.

"Me, too, Molls. I'll be in the den."

"Thanks, Dimitri." She smiled once more, her eyes dry again, and he walked toward the den, stuffing his hands into his pockets since he didn't know what else to do with them. Molly had closed the door for some reason, so as soon as he walked inside, his dog looked up, his eyes bright.

Captain had been lying on his rug—one that had originally been for the living room until the dog had made it his own and dragged it with him around the house. Molly had been so damn mad, but Dimitri hadn't been able to work up too much anger since Captain hadn't destroyed anything else in the house, just that area rug that he'd claimed as his. It could have been worse. Though when Dimitri had said that, Molly hadn't been too pleased with either of them.

Dimitri went to his knees as Captain bounded over to

him, sniffing, licking, and being so damn affectionate, Dimitri almost fell backwards.

"Hey, boy. I can't stay long, but I need you to eat some dinner. How about that?" Captain whined, licking Dimitri's face a few more times before going to his bowl and demolishing his food.

Dimitri let out a sigh, then moved over so he could sit by his dog and pet him as he ate. Of course, his damn dog had only wanted Dimitri's company and had used any means to get it. This would have to stop, though he had no idea how to make it happen. It was putting a strain on all of them, and he hated the fact that Captain wouldn't do certain things for Molly just because he missed Dimitri. He missed his dog, as well, but things were complicated.

Dimitri thought of Thea again.

So damn complicated.

He spent another twenty minutes with Captain before the golden finally fell asleep on his rug. Dimitri tiptoed out. He hated the whining that came when he had to leave, and it broke a little more of him every time he had to do it. It wasn't a fair situation for anyone, but for now, it was the way it had to be.

As he quietly made his way to the front door, Molly was there, her hands folded over her stomach.

"He's sleeping now."

"I gathered. He loves you so much, Dimitri."

He blew out a breath. "I know."

She walked up to him then, rubbing at his jaw with her

thumb. When it came back red—the same color lipstick Thea had been wearing—he held back his reaction.

"I'm glad you had fun tonight," she whispered.

He didn't say anything, couldn't. She might have guessed about Thea, or maybe thought he'd been with someone else after the party and before coming to her place for Captain. Dimitri didn't know, but he didn't have the words anyway.

He needed to talk to Thea.

Dimitri met Molly's eyes, gave her a nod, then walked out of the house, feeling as though he'd been kicked in the gut after burning everything around him.

One decision had changed everything, had possibly cost him more than he could bear. And yet as he thought of Thea, thought of what could happen next, he wasn't sure he'd have made another choice.

And that was something he'd have to think about as he waded his way through the tangled mess he currently found himself in. He just prayed he didn't break those he cared about in the process.

CHAPTER 8

Thea poured herself another glass of wine, trying not to go overboard like she had the night before. But two glasses while she was at home and not driving anywhere with her family and friends surrounding her wasn't a bad thing.

As long as she wasn't near Dimitri, she was fine.

Thea winced, trying not to think of him as she gulped down another sip. Though was it really a sip if she were gulping it down like a Lannister instead of a Montgomery? Did it really matter when she was probably going to have a third glass to sip casually soon?

No?

Okay, then.

"So, are you going to finish the whole bottle yourself, or are you going to share?" Adrienne asked from Thea's side, giving her a slight hip bump. "I mean, I can open the bottle of Riesling you have chilling, but I figured we'd all share the Malbec you opened first. Didn't know this was going to be a more-than-two-bottles kind of cooking date."

Thea met her sister's gaze and took another sip before setting her glass down. "I didn't drink the whole bottle."

Only a third. Whatever.

Kaylee, their friend and the art instructor for Brushes With Lushes, sashayed into the kitchen. The woman never just walked. She glided, she strutted, she flowed.

"I'll take that," Kaylee said with a wink as she plucked the bottle from Adrienne's hand.

"Hey!" Adrienne reached for the bottle, but Kaylee danced out of the way, pouring herself another glass.

"Apparently, we *will* be opening up more than two bottles."

Roxie just rolled her eyes. "Five women equals more than two bottles of wine, Thea. You should know that."

Abby stayed silent as she sipped her single glass, a smile playing on her lips. The other woman was still so quiet most days, but she was getting better at socializing. Hence why she was at Thea's house with the others for an early dinner and supposedly little drinking.

Supposedly.

"I figured we'd have more food than drinks but, apparently, I was wrong." Thea rolled her eyes before going back to the counter to start chopping up veggies for their stir-fry. Roxie started on the sauce, while Adrienne worked on the cheese plate. Thea, of course, monitored the cheeses but did her best not to make it look as if she were doing so. Cheese and stir-fry didn't always mix, but they were Montgomerys, and cheese was life, so it happened to make it into almost every group meal. They couldn't help it.

Abby and Kaylee worked on the rice and table settings, and the five of them laughed, drank more wine, and did their best not to burn themselves since they kept bumping into each other in the kitchen.

"So, Mace was trying to get Daisy to sleep, but Daisy decided to play a game of tag instead." Adrienne snorted. "So it's nine at night, and the little girl who I swear has never rambled before in her life, starts screaming with laughter and talking a mile a minute as she evades Mace while he chases her around the house."

Daisy was Mace's child from a previous relationship. Daisy's mother had moved to Japan for work and had given up custody so she could focus on her career and create a substantial college fund for Daisy. Thea had no idea what the other woman was thinking, but Mace and Adrienne were doing their best to make sure Daisy had the best life she could have. Mace's ex wasn't a horrible person—okay, maybe she was—but there was still communication and lots of letters and video chats between mother and daughter. Thea didn't know how that relationship could ever be fully repaired, but Daisy's mother cared in her own weird and dysfunctional way.

"And where were you during this?" Thea asked, pulling herself out of those thoughts.

"Laughing on the floor like any good girlfriend would be. Tears streaming down my face, giggling to the point where I couldn't breathe. You know, the usual." Adrienne beamed, and Thea held back a happy sigh. Her older sister was just so damn happy these days. She'd fallen in love with her best friend and had gotten a little girl who meant everything in the world to her in the process. Thea knew Mace and Adrienne had already talked about marriage but were taking things slowly since their relationship, once they'd started seeing one another, had gotten hot, fast.

Thea was only a little jealous. Not of Adrienne having Mace, but of the idea that someone could love another so quickly. Thea glanced over at Roxie, doing her best not to make it look like she was doing so. She loved Roxie and Carter together, but she wished she knew what that undercurrent of...sadness was that she always felt between the couple.

Or maybe she was just thinking too hard about it because she wasn't dating anyone anymore and doing her best not to think about Dimitri at all.

She took another sip that wasn't a sip but more of a gulp.

Adrienne gave her a look that meant there would be questions about her mood and actions soon, and Thea had a feeling there would be no running from it. After all, she'd done the same thing to her sister more than once.

By the time they'd finished making dinner and were all at the dining room table, laughing, eating, and drinking—water in Thea's case since she didn't want to go *too* overboard—Thea knew she couldn't hold back anymore.

It wasn't that anyone was interrogating her, far from it, but it was the anticipation of that interrogation and the fact that she truly needed to tell *someone* what happened that made her want to spill.

And it wasn't like she could talk about it with Molly.

Dear God.

"I slept with Dimitri."

She hadn't meant to blurt it out like that. Had meant to casually drop it into conversation with theoreticals and maybes. She didn't even plan to say his name or even mention it was her. She was going to be smart about it, maybe be casually hypothetical, and try not to make it sound like a big deal when it was truly one of the biggest deals.

Abby had her drink up to her lips, her eyes wide as she stared at Thea, but she didn't say a word. Kaylee had snorted her iced tea at the announcement and was currently blotting her top, a small smile playing on her lips, but she too remained silent. Adrienne tilted her head and blinked wildly, though she didn't speak either.

No, it was Roxie who spoke first.

"Like...fell asleep after a long night, or banging hard against something? Because Dimitri seems like the hard-banging type."

Thea couldn't help the laugh that burbled from her throat, and she slapped her hand over her mouth to stop herself.

But it was too late.

The others laughed as well before Adrienne tapped her wine glass with her knife, bringing everyone to attention.

"Thea didn't answer, so I'm going with banging." Her sister turned to her. "Am I right?"

Thea swallowed the rest of her water, and Abby quietly reached over to pour some more. Bless her.

"We had sex. On my living room floor."

There was a round of cheers as Abby asked, "When?"

Thea bit her lip. "After game night."

Roxie laughed. "I knew you two were competitive, but that's taking it to a whole new level."

Adrienne frowned. "Huh? How is banging on the floor competitive? Unless there's like a banging Olympics."

"Can we please refrain from using the word *banging*?" Thea asked, rubbing her temple. "It wasn't...*banging*."

"Sex is good for the soul," Kaylee said sagely, her lips still fighting that smile. "Or so I hear."

"You're a gorgeous artist with a fantastic rack," Adrienne put in, "I'm sure you get all the sex you want."

In answer, Kaylee toasted with her tea before downing the whole thing.

Interesting.

"We'll get back to that soon," Roxie said before turning to Thea. "You slept with Dimitri. As in your best friend's ex-husband, Dimitri. Am I getting that right?"

Guilt swarmed Thea, and she nodded slowly, wishing she hadn't had so much to eat since she was afraid it was all going to come up again. She was a horrible friend, a horrible person in general. And she hated herself the more she thought about exactly what she'd done.

"Yes, that's right. I slept with Dimitri. My friend. The

same friend who used to be married to my other friend. I'm going to hell."

"No, you aren't," Abby said. "There are codes or whatever gibberish the media tells us, but that doesn't mean they aren't murky."

"How exactly did it happen?" Roxie asked, then put up her hands as the others glared at her. "I don't need the details, though you know us, we always want the details since we're fiends like that. But, really, you two were a little buzzed but totally not drunk when the rest of us left. You guys were warm and laughing and acting like the friends we all know you are. Hell, Dimitri looked lighter than I've ever seen him, actually. Like he was *happy*. So, what happened?"

"He dared me to a rematch of Twister, and when one foot went one way, and the other foot the other, we ended up tangled up in one another and then…and then, well…"

"Over Twister?" Roxie gasped.

"What game was it supposed to be?" Adrienne asked dryly. "Dungeons and Dragons?"

Roxie affected her most serious face. "Is that not how you defeat the troll?"

This sent everyone at the table into peals of laughter, but Thea could only look down at her clasped hands.

Abby reached out and put her hand on top of hers and gave a squeeze. "Don't beat yourself up. You had sex with a single man. That's it."

"It's more than that, and we all know it. I slept with a man who used to be married to my best friend."

Adrienne scowled and sipped her drink.

"What?" Thea asked. "What's that look for."

"I don't know. You call Molly your best friend, and yet she doesn't hang out with us. We don't even know the woman. But, whatever."

"And that gives me an excuse to sleep with her ex?" Thea asked, incredulous.

"No, you don't need an excuse. And one has nothing to do with the other. But I've never liked that *best friend* tag you've given her."

"I agree," Roxie put in.

Thea just shook her head. "Whatever you think, she's still my friend. Just because she's not an honorary Montgomery like Mace doesn't mean she's not my friend."

"I get that. But I also think you're putting too much guilt on your shoulders for a woman who doesn't give you anything." Adrienne winced and then shook her head. "I'm sorry. I'm off track and, apparently, one glass of wine makes me say things that shouldn't be said."

Thea wasn't so sure that was all it was since the others were staring at Thea as if their minds were on the same track as her sister's. Just because Thea and Molly didn't run in the same circles or see each other every week, and their families weren't close, didn't make their friendship any less.

Damn it.

"I don't know what to do, you guys." Thea rested her face in her hands, and Abby rubbed small circles over Thea's back.

"You need to talk to her," Adrienne said softly. "If it's

hurting you this much, you need to talk to her. But before you do, you need to talk to Dimitri to see what it all meant."

Thea looked up, narrowing her eyes. "It meant nothing. It can't mean anything. He's my friend, just like Molly is. Having sex with him was a drunken mistake that can't happen again." And though it hurt to say those words, she knew they had to be true, because she couldn't lose both of her friends because of her actions.

It didn't matter that Dimitri was the best sex she'd ever had and that he meant more to her than she could say because it all had to be ignored. She had to keep her friends, no matter what.

"I've seen the two of you together," Adrienne said after a moment. "There's something there, Thea."

Thea was already shaking her head before her sister had finished speaking. "There can't be."

"Then talk to them both and make sure everything is out in the open," Roxie said. "Secrets kill, Thea."

There was something in her sister's words that worried Thea, but she didn't say anything. It was already enough as it was. So, she took a deep breath and tried to think about what she was going to do next. Because no matter what, she couldn't lie to Molly, and while she knew that sleeping with Dimitri had been a mistake, she still cared about him and couldn't push him out of her life completely.

To say that things were complicated was an understatement.

But she'd figure it out. Because she had to. There wasn't another choice.

CHAPTER 9

*T*hea sat in her car in front of Molly's house, knowing she needed to send out the text she'd been dreading now, or it would be too late.

Thea: *I need to tell Molly what happened.*

Dimitri answered right away, telling her he'd been close to his phone just like she had been all day. The girls had left after dinner, and Thea had called Molly, telling her that they needed to talk. The wine was out of her system, and Thea would be doing this stone-cold sober. Dimitri hadn't contacted her all day, but she figured he wouldn't. She'd been the one to kick him out of the house, and she'd known that he would never push her into contact. That wasn't the man he was.

If he hadn't been Molly's first...well, then, maybe things

would be different between the two of them. But they weren't, and Thea would just have to deal.

Dimitri: *Okay. I didn't want to tell her until I talked with you.*

Dimitri: *But, Thea? She noticed lipstick on my jaw, and I don't know if she thought it was you or another woman. Just be prepared. And I'm sorry.*

Dimitri: *Not sorry it happened, but sorry you have to do this.*

Thea sucked in a breath, her hands shaking. So, Molly might already suspect. And while Thea technically hadn't done anything wrong, it still felt icky. So, she'd tell Molly everything and take whatever the other woman gave her. She deserved nothing less.

Thea: *Thank you.*

Dimitri: *We should talk.*

Thea: *Not yet.*

Dimitri: *Soon.*

Thea didn't answer. Instead, she slid her phone into her purse before getting out of the car. Time to face the music and whatever else came with it. She knew that while she hadn't really done anything wrong, she'd still done *every-*

thing wrong. It didn't matter what feelings might be, at this very moment, curling inside her, she had to tamp those down since they had no place in her life, especially not when friendship meant more than anything.

It had to, or she wasn't the woman she thought she was.

Thea knocked on the door, and Molly opened it quickly. "Hey there. I'm glad you stopped by." Molly smiled and leaned over, giving Thea a tight hug that made Thea want to hide.

She was a terrible friend with terrible decision-making skills. But she'd tell Molly the truth, and whatever happened after that, she'd deal with.

"Thanks for letting me come over on such short notice."

Molly waved her off. "No worries, darling. I had my mani-pedi earlier and was just working on the donation requests for the next fundraiser. So much to do, so little time. Though now you can help me pick out my outfit for the next event. I do love that part."

Thea smiled, but she knew it didn't reach her eyes. And, honestly, even if she weren't here to possibly ruin Molly's world, she hated picking out outfits for her friend. They had such different tastes, and Thea never understood the cutthroat nature of trying to one-up another at a charity function. However, it wasn't Thea's world, and since she was there for not-so-nice reasons as it was, she ignored that train of thought.

"Molly? There's something I need to tell you."

Her friend must have read something in Thea's tone

because she straightened, nodding slightly. "Okay, honey. What is it?"

"We should probably sit down."

"Now you're worrying me." But even as she said it, she sat on one of the ornate couches that Thea had always been worried about spilling something on, and she knew Dimitri had felt the same.

But, then again, he'd loved his wife and had let her pick out the things that filled their home. Everything except Captain, that was.

Speaking of… "Where's Captain?" Thea asked, not trying to change the subject but wanting to know. Usually, the beautiful golden met her at the door with kisses and love, but today, that had been suspiciously absent. Thea knew that Dimitri came over often to be with his dog and to get him to eat or go on walks, so she just hoped that Captain was okay.

Molly waved her off. "He's at the groomer's. Just a wash and a good brushing since Dimitri says you don't shave goldens. But the hair, Thea. So much hair."

Thea tried to imagine a shaved golden retriever and held back a wince. It wouldn't be a good look. Thea hadn't known Captain ever went to the groomer's, but then again, she didn't know everything about what went on with Captain, it wasn't any of her business.

"What is it you wanted to tell me, dear?"

Thea took a deep breath. "Something happened at game night, Molly."

Her friend didn't say anything, but a small frown marred her otherwise perfect face.

"Dimitri came over, and I guess we had a little too much to drink." Though that hadn't been the reason she'd let herself fall, but she couldn't tell Molly that. It wouldn't make sense to either of them if she did. "One thing led to another, and...Molly, I'm so sorry, but Dimitri and I slept together. It was a one-time thing, and it'll never happen again. While Dimitri and I are friends, so are you and me. And I value what you and I have, Molly. You're my friend." Thea didn't say *best friend*. Adrienne's words were still ringing in her ears, but she ignored that. After all, if Thea were a true best friend, she wouldn't have slept with Dimitri in the first place.

"I'm so sorry, Molly. I never wanted to hurt you, but I'm afraid my careless actions might have done the worst. I'll never be able to forgive myself for what happened, for how I've broken the trust between us by stepping over that line. Dimitri has always been my friend, nothing more, and in doing what we did, we crossed a line. I broke your trust, and I'm so sorry."

Molly didn't say anything for so long that Thea was afraid the tears she was holding back would finally fall, and she'd end up sobbing on the floor, begging Molly to forgive her. But she wouldn't do that. She wouldn't debase any of them by ruining what little pride she had left by demanding acceptance from a woman who didn't have any to offer. It didn't matter that Molly and Dimitri didn't love each other anymore. They once had, and that was all that mattered.

They had belonged to one another, and it had nothing to do with Thea.

It *should* have nothing to do with Thea.

And she would make sure that was the truth.

Finally, Molly smiled brightly, startling Thea, and said, "Did you do anything before the divorce?"

"No. Of course, not." Thea's eyes went wide. "I never even thought about him in that way. He was always yours."

"Then, no harm, no foul." Molly shrugged.

Thea blinked. Had she heard right?

"We just didn't work out, dear. We're not that kind of couple, you know?"

Thea didn't know. In fact, she had no idea how to possibly comprehend how well Molly was taking this.

"And I can't begrudge my best friend for finding happiness. Any form of happiness. And by *best friend*, I mean you both."

Molly smiled again, and Thea's heart clutched. *Both.* Her best friends were Dimitri and Thea. How complicated and tangled and yet utterly monstrous for Thea to even be here in this room asking for forgiveness.

"I love you both so much. Just not in the way I should have when it came to Dimitri. He and I are over. And oddly, it seems like fate that it's a new beginning for the two people I cherish most in my life."

Thea was confused, so damn confused. "What? There's no new beginning, Molly. It was…it wasn't what you think."

Molly continued on as if Thea hadn't said anything. Not

that it was unusual when it came to Molly, but Thea felt as if she were behind in this conversation.

"If there's anything I can do, I'm here. I might not have been the wife Dimitri needed, but at some point, we were what we *thought* we needed. So maybe, just maybe, I can help you."

Thea held up her hand, finding it shaking. "It was just that one time, Molly, it doesn't mean what you're thinking."

Molly just gave her a placating smile. "Well, if I know Dimitri, and you know I do, then that one time might just be a little more." The other woman winked. *Winked.* "And, really, with the way he moves, I'm sure you know what I'm talking about."

Thea laughed woodenly as the other woman continued, but she couldn't help the nerves welling up inside her.

How had she ended up here?

Was Molly really okay with things progressing between her and Dimitri? And what the hell was she going to do now when it came to a certain inked teacher that she'd thought might be out of her life forever?

Because Molly was acting weird, so damn weird. And Thea had no idea what to do about it, what to believe, or what to hope for.

Once again, she knew this called for wine, and even Thea didn't know if she had enough of it.

CHAPTER 10

*D*imitri put his hands on his hips, trying not to glare at the kid in front of him. But, damn it, he was just so disappointed that he'd had to talk himself out of so many different variations of how this conversation might go.

One of his brightest kids was failing his class, and there was nothing Dimitri could do about it beyond what he was doing now. He hated the fact that this was out of his grasp and it was going to take time—and maybe even a miracle—for things to change.

But he'd try his damnedest to make that happen because all of his students deserved the best, *his* best.

"Jason."

The kid lifted his head, his dark hair falling in front of his face in a messy array of angles and random cuts. Apparently, the shaggy haircut was a new trend or something. The fact that it almost mirrored Dimitri's, only messier, wasn't lost on him.

"I need you to complete your assignments. You used to do so last year, and when you moved up to this grade with your peers, you stopped doing them. Tell me what's wrong, Jason. Let me try to help."

Jason shrugged. "I'm fine."

Dimitri held back a sigh and walked around the desk separating them to lean on the side. "No, you're not fine. I'm going to call a parent-teacher conference, and I know you're going to hate it. But I know you understand the material. I see the way your eyes move during class." And how Jason mouthed the answers even if he didn't raise his hand to answer out loud. Dimitri didn't push all of his students to speak every day like some teachers. He knew most needed their own quiet space, and those he thought weren't paying attention were the ones he called on. It usually meant that everyone was at least trying.

Trying when it came to participation, that was.

Turning in assignments? Jason wasn't the only holdout, but he was the most dramatic turn when It came to his grades, and Dimitri was going to do his best to find out why.

"I don't need a meeting."

"You might not. But I do. Is there something going on at home you want to talk about?"

"No. Everything's fine."

Even if Dimitri didn't know Jason's parents were going through a particularly nasty divorce, he'd have heard the lie in Jason's assertion. Colorado Springs was by no means a small town, but Jason's dad had moved into the same apartment complex Dimitri currently resided in. Apparently, all newly single men without homes knew it was the place to be.

Jesus, Dimitri needed to do something about his life, but first, he needed to try and do something about Jason's.

"We're going to talk, Jason. All of us. But in the meantime, if you need anything. I'm here."

"Whatever. Are we done now?"

While he didn't like Jason's attitude, there was nothing Dimitri could do about it now, so he let the kid leave, shaking his head as he looked down at his notes. Jason could be an *A* student, but things had changed, and Dimitri wanted to fix it.

But he'd been a teacher long enough to know that while he couldn't fix everything, he could at least try.

"Mr. Carr. Good, you're here. We need to talk."

Vice Principle Riley strode into Dimitri's classroom, his chin raised, and his signature sneer in place like usual. Dimitri didn't know how the guy had worked his way up the ranks, but for some reason, Dimitri could never seem to do anything right in the guy's eyes.

That's what happened when he looked the part of a rock star—at least according to Riley—rather than a staid teacher.

What the fuck ever.

"What can I do for you?"

"You can keep those sleeves down. I don't need any more complaints about your attire."

Dimitri looked down at his sleeves that completely covered his ink. He didn't even need to pull them down, but he gave Riley a bland look.

"My tattoos are covered. You shouldn't be getting any complaints."

"We'll see."

With that, Riley strode out of the room, and Dimitri rolled his neck. He was seriously starting to hate his job and knew that if things didn't change, he'd have to find a new school where he could be who he was. It hadn't been a problem before, the people changing with the times and tattoos not being a problem at most of the schools he'd taught at. He just hoped Riley got his stick out of his ass soon so Dimitri wouldn't have to make yet another life-altering decision.

Of course, if he changed schools, he'd have to change houses, too. But maybe then he'd be able to get one where he could have Captain with him rather than their current situation.

The thought of moving made him think of not being near Thea, and he shook his head as he packed up his things. He hadn't heard from her except for her texts after she'd left Molly's saying the deed was done. She'd ignored his request to talk, and he'd let her have that as he wasn't going to fucking stalk her.

The fact that Molly hadn't texted him yet either worried him, but not enough for him to freak out. He had enough on his plate, and he needed to have a clear head for work and, frankly, to figure out what he was going to do when it came to Thea Montgomery.

He'd do that. But first, he had dinner. Mace had invited him out for a drink and wings with the guys, and since Dimitri didn't really have a set of friends of his own, he'd jumped at the chance. Sure, things were already complicated when it came to Thea, and going out with her sister's guy for a drink might make it weird. But Dimitri needed friends that weren't part of Molly's circle, and after hanging out with Carter and Mace at Thea's, he liked the two and wanted to see if something could work out between them all.

Look at him, turning over new leaves everywhere he went.

Since his meetings had run late, he didn't have time to go home or even stop by Molly's to see Captain before he headed to the bar. Not that he was looking forward to seeing Molly after her conversation with Thea. But it would have to happen sometime, and he'd face the consequences of his actions when it did. He just hoped that Molly hadn't taken out any anger she might have on Thea.

Thea didn't deserve that. If anyone did, it was Dimitri. Sure, he was a single man who could sleep with and date anyone he chose, but that didn't mean he should take anyone's feelings lightly.

It wasn't lost on him that the first person he'd slept with after his divorce was Thea. He hadn't been interested in any form of relationship with another person so soon after his divorce when he first moved into his apartment. In the months since the divorce, he'd noticed women, but he hadn't been in the mood to start anything new.

That was until he saw Thea again.

He had no idea what exactly he wanted—*if* she ever spoke to him again—but he knew that he didn't want their connection, whatever it was, to end. How that would work, he didn't know, but he had a feeling he'd soon find out.

As he pulled into the parking lot of the local wing place Mace loved, Dimitri put those thoughts to the side since he really didn't want to talk about it with the guys. It seemed Mace and his friends came here often enough that it was *their place,* and Dimitri was oddly excited.

He was starting a new phase of his life in more ways than one it seemed.

Mace and another man Dimitri didn't recognize were already seated at a table when Dimitri made his way to the back.

Mace raised his hand in greeting, and the other guy lifted his chin. "Hey, glad you made it, Dimitri. This is Landon. He's a friend from way back, and now works at the most boring job possible."

Landon, a slender man with dark hair and sharp looks, flipped his friend off before holding out a hand. "I'm a broker. Sorry, I'm not a famous tattoo artist who gets to play with sharp objects all day."

Dimitri snorted and shook the other man's hand before taking a seat. "I'm a high school math teacher. Not quite sure I live up to Mace's expectations of a non-boring job either."

Mace rolled his eyes, taking a sip of his beer. "Still better than playing with other people's money."

"Numbers are numbers," Landon said, saluting Dimitri with his beer. "Am I right?"

"I'm with Landon on this one," Dimitri said with a laugh, and Mace just shook his head at both of them.

"I can't with you two. When Ryan and Carter get here, at least I won't be outnumbered. Pun not intended. Now, pour yourself a beer, Dimitri. We do cheap pitchers since it's happy hour and will order massive amounts of whatever's on special for wings. That okay with you?"

Dimitri shrugged as he poured himself a glass. "Sounds good to me. I'm not picky."

Landon sighed. "You should be. The wings are phenomenal, no matter the sauce, but one day I'd like for us to actually have *taste* when it comes to what we're drinking."

"And we do on other nights. Tonight's about cheap beer and wings and trying not to overdo it since none of us are in our early twenties anymore." Mace gave a mock shiver. "Heartburn is not my friend."

Dimitri raised his glass at that. "Amen, brother."

The waitress came by for their order, and Mace spoke for them all, getting more wings of various flavors than Dimitri thought they could all eat but, apparently, the crew had a rhythm. By the time she left to get another pitcher for the table, the last two of their party had made their way in.

Dimitri knew both of them, though not well. He'd met

Carter a few times since the other man had married Thea's sister, Roxie, but they hadn't spoken all that much until game night.

He tried not to think about game night because then he couldn't help but think of Thea.

And he was *not* going to think about Thea tonight.

Much.

He quickly looked at the other man taking a seat at the table so he could clear his thoughts. Dimitri knew Ryan from Montgomery Ink Too, the new tattoo shop in the Montgomery family. He'd talked to the man a few times and would soon be in to get more ink, though, likely, it would be Adrienne or Mace who did the actual tattooing.

"Oh, hey, Dimitri, glad you could make it," Ryan said, lifting his chin. "Sorry I'm late. Took forever to get the last client out the door."

Mace frowned. "Ethan, right? He has a crush on you, I think."

Ryan sighed. "Yup. I tried to go easy on him and let him down nicely, but it's not working out."

"Didn't you used to date his friend, Jack?" Landon asked, sipping his beer.

"Yeah, and that's the problem. I know Ethan through Jack, and I know how…I don't want to say clingy, but maybe obsessive he can get. Plus, he just doesn't ring my bell."

"I thought you were dating Angie?" Mace asked while Dimitri sat back in his chair, listening to a conversation he knew no part of but liking learning about new people anyway.

"I was. Now, I'm not. We were just casual anyway. Plus, the fact that Ethan doesn't believe I'm bi and thinks that I'm going through a phase or some shit about not being able to make a choice annoys the fuck out of me."

Carter frowned. "Then why did you say you'd do his tattoo? Seems like it wouldn't be a good idea." The other man poured himself and Ryan beers, and the younger tattoo artist chugged half of his back before answering.

"Because I thought I'd do the right thing and not say no because of personal shit."

"Don't do that again," Mace warned. "You know Shep and Adrienne will have your balls if you do work you're not comfortable with. Any of the rest of us will take the job, or the guy doesn't get in the shop. We can turn people away if the situation merits it."

Mace's eyes clouded for a moment, and Dimitri had a feeling the other man was thinking about the close call Adrienne had gone through just a few short weeks ago. Adrienne was fine now, but she hadn't been at first—none of them had been after hearing about the attack.

"I know what you're thinking about, and that was different," Ryan put in before holding up his hands. "But I get you. No more jobs that make work uncomfortable."

"Good." Mace nodded before taking another sip. "And here are our wings. They're fast tonight."

Since Dimitri's stomach had just rumbled, he was glad for it. Everyone dug in with gusto, Dimitri going for the mid-grade hotness since he liked the heat but didn't want to hate himself later for it.

Ryan and Carter each went for the ultra-spicy, but neither of them looked as if they were feeling any effects. At least, not yet. As both were only a few years younger than Dimitri, he didn't know how they did it.

"I thought Shep was coming," Landon said, licking parmesan from his fingers.

"Livvy has a cold, so he's home with Shea."

"Poor kid," Ryan said. "Glad to have Shep back in town, though."

"I didn't know you knew him from before he moved down to New Orleans," Dimitri said.

"I didn't, but Adrienne and the others are happier, so I'm happy, too."

Dimitri nodded, agreeing. He hadn't liked when Thea's brother was so far away because Thea had always been close to Shep, all the girls had. It was nice that all the Montgomerys were together again.

"How's the shop?" Dimitri asked Carter since the other man was seated right next to him. Carter was a mechanic who owned and operated his own place and, apparently, worked long-as-hell hours. Dimitri had no idea how the other man juggled that and a new marriage, but then again, Dimitri had been teaching long hours and grading endless papers while learning to be a husband at first, too. It hadn't worked out that well for Dimitri. He hoped to hell Carter was doing a better job of it.

"Busy as usual, but I hired a new guy so I can try to take weekends off." The other man shrugged. "We'll see. Though around tax season, I might just go back to weekends since Roxie won't be home anyway."

Roxie was an accountant and worked just as many hours as Carter did it seemed, but Dimitri liked the idea that the other man was trying.

"I guess when I need a tune-up I should go somewhere else?" he asked with a grin.

Carter pointed at him with a wing. "You go anywhere else, I'll hunt you down."

"You're one of us now," Mace said. "You're stuck."

Dimitri just smiled before eating more wings. One of them? He could deal with that. It had been far too long since he'd had a group of friends like this, and maybe, just maybe, this could work out.

He just hoped whatever was happening with Thea coincided with that.

TWO BEERS and far too many wings later, Dimitri was home alone on his couch, wishing to hell and back that he had his dog with him. *That will change soon,* he thought. It had to. Because this separation wasn't good for either of them.

He looked down at his phone, the beer totally out of his system, and knew he needed to make the first move in whatever the hell was going to happen next—and not with Captain.

Dimitri: *Hey.*

He sucked at texting, sucked at words. He was a math teacher. Give him numbers and a problem to solve, and he'd do just fine. Finding out what to say when it came to a woman he cared about when he wasn't sure what he wanted or what *could* happen between them?

Total cluelessness.

Thea: *Hey.*

She texted back. That had to count for something, right? And...now he'd turned into one of his students, overanalyzing a damn text and the recipient's response time.

Dimitri: *Went out with the guys tonight. Had wings.*

Thea: *The guys?*

Dimitri: *Mace, Ryan, Landon, and Carter.*

He frowned.

Dimitri: *Was that okay? Hanging out with your sisters' guys?*

Thea: *Of course it's okay. I know you said you wanted friends outside your old circle. It shouldn't matter what I think anyway.*

They were both careful not to mention Molly's name. Oh, so careful.

Dimitri: *Of course it matters what you think. You know that.*

She didn't answer, and he was afraid he'd fucked up again.

Dimitri: *Have coffee with me.*

Dimitri: *Please.*

Thea: *I make coffee for a living. I'm good.*

Dimitri: *You make the best coffee. Let's drink it together.*

If she said no this time, he wouldn't ask again, wouldn't badger her. But he needed to at least try.

She was silent for so long, he was afraid of the answer.

Thea: *Tomorrow.*

He let out a breath and asked the time, then set his phone down after saying goodnight. He had a coffee date with Thea tomorrow, a real one. It had to be a date, not just friends, but not more than that either. Time where they could find their boundaries and decide what they each wanted.

It seemed a lot for a single cup of coffee, no matter how good she made it.

He rested his head against the couch, knowing he was doing the right thing. He wasn't just hoping anymore. Thea meant something to him. This feeling she gave him, the look on her face when they were together even for a short time... it meant something. They'd figure out what was between them and work from there.

But he couldn't run away, wouldn't hide anymore.

He was a new man, a new Dimitri. Now, he just needed to figure out exactly what that meant.

CHAPTER 11

*T*hea wanted to dive into her bowl of frosting, and she didn't care who noticed. If she could live in this creamy goodness, she would. She'd lick it all up, heavy breathing while she let it settle, then make some more so she could do it all again.

She and her sisters joked that she had extra curves because of all her baked goods—tasting was important, after all—but she secretly knew that it wasn't from the cakes and cookies and tarts. Oh, no, the extra padding on her ass came from the frosting, and she was just fine with it. Sure, she had to watch her sugar intake, and she ate healthily other- wise—if she ignored cheese— but she was in love with frosting.

Hence why she had to hold herself back. She didn't need clogged arteries or diabetes thanks to her love of frosting and cheese, but she also let herself indulge sometimes.

And the fact that today's special frosting was cream cheese? She was in dairy heaven and never wanted to leave.

Thea didn't exactly lick the spoon she'd been using, but she did sniff at it, imagining the sweet and slightly tangy taste on her tongue. Not only was licking anything in her kitchen at work against code, but she needed every ounce of the frosting for her red velvet cheesecake cupcakes.

They were hot sellers this time of year—hell, *every* time of year—and it was all she could do not to make so many of them that even she got sick of the glorious bombs of sugar and flavor. They were her favorite thing on the menu, and because of that, she never had one. They were for her customers, and she'd eat a carrot or something while imagining it was frosting.

Not the best thing in the world, but it was better for her ass and her blood sugar.

While she let the frosting rest a bit before she topped the cupcakes, she went to the oven to pull out her pastries, letting them cool before she put on the fruit toppings. The oven dinged again, and she slid out her rolls and the other bread items that were done and ready to go for the day. Her early morning to-do list had a few more things on it like frosting the cakes and decorating for certain private orders, but she'd get to that once the shop was fully open for the day.

She had two of her staff coming in soon to help out with the finishing touches and to work the counter, but this morning, she was on her own. She didn't mind. Frankly, it was one of her favorite times of the day, where she surrounded herself with the things that she'd made by hand. These were times and baked goods that were all hers and had something to do with her future. With her own creativity and talent in her chosen career, she'd been able to buy a house, keep it, keep her bakery doors open, *and* make it flourish.

And, soon, if everything worked out and the baking gods smiled down on her, she'd be able to reach the next phase of her multi-step baking plan.

Because, of course, she had one of those color-coded with checkboxes, but her personal life had no such list. It didn't matter, though, because she was doing better at that by working on the fly.

She held back a laugh. Okay, not so much, since she was beyond floundering when it came to her personal life.

Roger was totally gone from her life and thoughts, not even worth a second glance since there was no way she'd debase herself like that again. Dimitri, however?

She took a steadying breath, bracing herself against the metal counter. Okay, so maybe she was a little lost there, but something was going to change today.

He was coming in for coffee this afternoon after school, and that meant they were going to *talk*. They were going to discuss what happened between them and see where they could go next.

Molly was all for it. Frankly, that worried Thea a bit. What had her friend meant when she said she wanted Dimitri and Thea to work out? It all seemed so surreal, and she and Dimitri truly needed to talk.

Because even if everything else went to hell, she still wanted to have him in her life. She'd come to that conclusion the night before. She wanted him as her friend. At least her friend.

And that meant talking to him over coffee as the first step.

The first step to what, though, she didn't know. But it was at least something.

Thea pushed those thoughts to the side, though she knew they would be on her mind all day, and went about getting ready to open the bakery. Since they were the first stop for many people on their way to work, she had horribly early hours according to her sister, but Thea had learned long ago to adjust her body to bakers' hours.

Both of her staff members came in on time, and soon, the place was bustling with people on their way to work in need of caffeine and sugar. Thea had a few healthier options like fruit and whole grains, but mostly, it was all about the bread and pastries this morning. When her next phase began, she'd have healthier options for sure, but first, she needed to get to that part. That wasn't for today, however, since they were busy, and she had countless specialty coffee orders to fill.

By mid-morning, the lines hadn't died down, and Thea couldn't help but smile. She *loved* her job and loved the fact that her life's dream meant she could earn a living. They were still bustling as Abby walked into the place, holding two cups of hot tea that Thea knew would be divine.

When Abby had moved into the building a few doors

down with her tea shop, Teas'd, Thea hadn't felt like the other woman was encroaching on her territory at all. In fact, the two of them had not only become friends but almost business partners. They weren't anywhere near something official, but they had a great working relationship.

Thea mostly did coffee and baked goods, but the tea she had on site was from Abby's place. And any baked goods Abby had at her place were from Thea's bakery. Teas'd was where one could buy loose leaf tea in bulk or just sit for a single cup or take one to-go. Abby also sold handmade teapots and other accessories made by local artists. Apparently, one of them was married to Thea's cousin.

It seemed Colorado was a lot smaller than Thea thought.

"I brought tea," Abby said with a grin. "I'm sure you had like four cups of coffee already, but I have a new blend of white chocolate and other goodies that I wanted you to try."

Thea's mouth watered, and she held out her hands. "Gimme."

Abby just laughed and handed over the mug, no paper cups for the two of them if they could help it.

As soon as Thea blew over the surface of the tea and took her first sip, she knew she was in Heaven. "Oh my God. What's in this?"

"A new rooibos blend I'm trying out. I'll give you the specs if you decide you want it in the shop."

Thea nodded, sipping some more. "I'm in love. And, hell yeah I want it in the shop. It's perfect for the season. Oh, and I have some of those cream cheese-frosted, red velvet cheesecake cupcakes you love if you want a dozen for the shop today."

Abby groaned. "Maybe only a half dozen or I'll eat them all and end up rolling around and not serving tea."

"That's my problem with them, as well." Thea winked, setting down her mug. The bakery was slowing a bit before the mid-afternoon rush, and she was grateful. It gave her time to get other things done around the place. "Want me to walk them over to you, and we can grab some lunch?"

Abby looked over her shoulder. "If you can swing it, sure. I actually brought my own sandwich today since I'm on a budget."

Abby never hid that she was still at the beginning stages of her business, and as a single mother, every penny counted. As Thea was possibly about to make more than one significant life change, she totally agreed.

"I brought in a sandwich, too," she said with a laugh. "I think I know us too well. I bet Adrienne brought hers too if we want to stop by and see if she has time."

During lunch times, the bakery sold a small variety of sandwiches with their baked bread, but they weren't equipped enough to do full salads or soups yet. That would change, though. At least, Thea hoped.

One thing at a time.

And that one thing was her coffee *date* that afternoon. Not that she was going to mention it to Adrienne and Abby during lunch. Not at all. She needed to keep this to herself, at least as much as she could for now while she figured out what she was doing. Yes, they all knew—including Molly—

what had happened, but the next stop should be hers and Dimitri's.

Maybe.

Everything was far too complicated, and she really needed one of those damn cupcakes. And because she was a glutton for gluttony today, she grabbed three of them for their dessert along with the six for Teas'd and headed out of Colorado Icing, leaving her staff in charge. They were good at what they did and handled the place expertly. She worked long hours because she loved it, not because she had to anymore.

Adrienne did have time to eat with them and she had brought lunch with her, so the three of them took one of Abby's tables in front of Teas'd. Abby only had two bistro tables. Thea had four. And though they needed more for good-weather days, until something changed, that wasn't going to happen.

Plans first, she thought. Then, they'd see.

By the time they finished their lunch and talked about the tattoo Adrienne was working on, as well as Abby's new tea, Thea was ready to head back to work, a container of tea in her hand for brewing. She could already smell the sweetness and couldn't wait to serve it in her shop. The day Abby came to Colorado Springs had been a blessing, even if Thea knew it had come from a place of heartbreak.

That wasn't Thea's story, however, so she never pried. She just hoped that one day, Abby would want to tell Thea the whole tale, at least to lessen that burden from the other woman's shoulders.

Thea was working on setting up a display case when Molly walked in, all class and bright smiles, looking ready for the runway and not what most people would be doing in Colorado Springs at this time of day—working or running errands. But since Molly always looked like that, sometimes even at home, it didn't really surprise Thea.

What *did* surprise Thea was that Molly was actually here in her shop so soon after everything had happened. Thea was still on the fence whether the conversation she'd had with the other woman was a dream or not. It wasn't as if Thea had time to ponder what it all meant. However, since Molly was walking toward her, Thea needed to act like nothing was wrong.

Not that anything *was* wrong, but Dimitri was coming into the shop soon for coffee—either just as friends or perhaps something more. She really didn't know but knew they needed to talk about it. The last thing anyone needed was the three of them in the same room in public before they all figured out what was going on. It was getting to be a little too much for Thea, and complicated wasn't a good enough word to describe it.

"Thea, darling, I'm so glad I caught you. I didn't know if you were working this afternoon, but from the flour in your hair, I'm assuming yes." Molly winked as if it were a joke, and Thea supposed it was. She was always covered in flour.

She winced and reached up to her bangs before lowering her hand. Sadly, she knew from experience that the more she messed with the flour in her dark hair, the more it would spread and make her look like a skunk. Plus, she was a bit sweaty from working all day even in the cooler air, and flour and water made paste. Having that in her hair was never a good thing.

"That's me, the flour queen. Do you want your usual, Molly?"

"A sugar-free, fat-free, vanilla latte please," her friend said with a smile. "Though, sometimes, I wish I could be as daring as you and go for full-sugar along with one of those brownies in front of you. They look delicious, but they also go right to my hips."

Thea just rolled her eyes and went about making Molly's drink. "As they *do* go to my hips, I don't indulge all the time. I mostly taste-test to make sure I have the recipe right." She kept her hands busy making the drink, her back to Molly, but she looked over her shoulder once in a while to make sure there weren't any other customers in, like...the afore-mentioned Dimitri.

"Your hips look good with a little bit of curve to them. My hips, on the other hand, just don't carry that weight. I don't know how you do it, but you look wonderful with curves. Me? I have to watch everything I eat."

Thea just rolled her eyes as she served Molly her coffee. Thea didn't ring the drink up, and Molly didn't bother to open her purse. That was how it had always been, and Thea didn't care anymore. The curve comment, however, stung a bit. But she figured it was a compliment. Maybe.

"You look wonderful, and you know it. Where are you off to today?" Thea kept working, changing out stock and fluffing the display case for the late-afternoon sugar hounds. People needed their fix so they could get through the rest of the day, and she was grateful.

"Committee meeting, of course. So much to do, so little time. But the world needs me."

"That we do," Thea said, not lying. Molly had been her friend for years, had been there when she opened Colorado Icing and bought her house the same year. Thea had done it on her own and with her family, but Molly had been around as well, always eager to offer advice about how things should be done. It didn't matter that Thea hadn't taken any of that advice since she had her own vision and business plans, her friend had still offered it.

"Must be off, but when I have time, we should catch up. I'd love to hear about you and a certain teacher."

Thea froze, but Molly just waved her fingers before sauntering out of the bakery in her four-inch stilettos. It was going to ice later, and Thea wasn't sure how the woman could walk in those things in this—or any—weather, but women were strong and could do just about anything.

Though how Molly could be so okay with whatever might happen between Thea and Dimitri was something Thea couldn't quite comprehend. The other woman had basically—and easily—given Thea the okay to pursue a relationship with her ex-husband and even wanted to offer advice, yet Thea felt as if she were barely keeping up with all the changes.

Thea didn't know if she wanted a full relationship with Dimitri, she didn't know if she could handle that with her business and her life, yet Molly seemed to *want* it.

Thea's life had already changed so drastically, she was struggling to understand it all.

And because she'd apparently conjured him out of thin air, Dimitri was the next person to walk through the door. She didn't think he'd bumped into Molly outside since he only smiled at Thea, giving her that look that went straight to her lady parts. And now she wasn't thinking about her friend at all.

She was just thinking about Dimitri and what the hell she was going to do about him. And, just like that, he was in front of her, making her doubt her resolve.

"Hey there," Dimitri said softly, his voice that low, whiskey growl that sent shivers down her spine.

"Hey." Oh, good, she was back in high school, unable to form complete sentences. She cleared her throat and started over. "School's out for the day, I take it? How was it?"

Dimitri just shrugged and leaned against the counter as others milled about. The rush would be soon, but for now, all of her tables were full of happy customers eating sweets and bread and drinking hot drinks since the temperature was dropping outside.

"School's out for the weekend, which is nice. Soon, we'll be at winter break, and I can try to sleep in a bit. It'll be interesting."

"Sleeping in? Like to seven or something?" she asked, her eyes wide.

He was the one to wince this time. "Oh, yeah, bakers' hours. I mean, I wake up early as hell to work out before work, but I think you beat me."

She smiled, but her brain was going a mile a minute thinking about Dimitri all sweaty, working out.

Shirtless.

With those shorts that rode low on his hips so she could see those lickable lines on either side of his body.

And that was enough of that.

When she met Dimitri's gaze, she figured he knew *exactly* what she was thinking, considering the heated look that passed between them.

Well, hell.

"Can you spare some time for coffee with me? I know you're working so I'm not going to force you into it. The fact that you're letting me into the building at all is a step."

"I wouldn't force you out of Colorado Icing."

"Maybe not, but you'd be so polite about it that it would hurt to know that I broke what we had."

She looked behind him, then gestured for one of her staff to mind the counter. "Come back to the office with me."

His brows rose, but he followed.

"Sorry, I know most of the people in here since they're all regulars, and while I don't want to hide anything, even if there ends up being nothing between us, I also don't need to advertise my personal life."

"Understandable, I'm a teacher. I get it. But I hope there's not nothing between us." He sighed. "I hate double negatives."

"They sometimes work, though. As for what you said back there... It wouldn't have been you that broke what we had. It would have been the two of us together. I hope you realize that."

Then she took a deep breath and told him exactly what Molly had said when they talked. The comically wide eyes on his face made her lips twitch even as she totally understood his reaction.

"Seriously? I...I don't get it."

"I don't either, but I also can't find a reason why she'd lie. Not even to cover up any hurt. She'd have said something like she was fine with it, but she wouldn't have actively put us together in her response. Or at least tried to."

Dimitri reached out and brushed his knuckle along Thea's cheek, and the fact that she didn't pull away spoke volumes about what her decision might be when it came to him.

"She's not part of *this*, not really. And while I don't want to hurt her, I think we both need to understand that."

She nodded at his words, letting out a slow breath. "But I don't know what *this* is."

"Then that's something we need to figure out." He paused. "I'm not in love with Molly, Thea. I haven't been in a long time. Too long, frankly. We aren't married anymore, and the only reason I see her is because of Captain. I don't hate her, I don't dislike her, but she's also not really a part of my life. I know she is a part of yours, and it might be hard to juggle that, so whatever you need from me, I can do. But there's something between us. I can feel it. I won't be an ass and say I know you feel it, too, because I'm not going to assume or tell you your feelings. But what I can say is that I don't think what happened between us was a mistake. I think that, eventually, without booze and without Twister, we would have fallen into each other like we did anyway. Or, at least that's what I wanted. So, what do you say, Thea? Will you take a chance on me?"

Thea pressed her lips together before giving him a slow nod. "I think...I think I have to, even as we try to be careful."

Dimitri immediately relaxed, his shoulders lowering, though he still had his hand on her face. "Good."

Then he lowered his head, his lips pressing firmly against hers, and she opened for him, wanting more, craving more.

She had no sugar in her system to blame, no booze.

This was all her and Dimitri.

All heat, tongues, and heavy breaths.

Dimitri bit her lower lip, and she shivered, arching into him even though he wasn't fully touching her. When he took a step toward her, coming so close she could feel the heat of him against her, she took an involuntary step back, needing to breathe. His presence was so large, it made her knees shake.

That one step pressed her lower back and butt against her desk, and she sucked in a breath. His eyes danced as he moved even closer, the slight gap between them a thing of the past as he lowered his head and took her mouth again. She was caught, locked in place, and melting into him all at once.

She wanted him, needed more of him, and couldn't help but wrap her arms around his neck and part her lips for him. She wanted to slide up on top of her desk and part her *legs*, but she knew they didn't have time for that.

Not yet.

But soon.

When they parted and went to the front for coffee, she knew it was a step—a huge one that wasn't that big at all.

She didn't know what was to come, but Dimitri was right, there *was* something between them. She just hoped that despite Molly's blessing, she didn't ruin it all.

CHAPTER 12

*B*rushes With Lushes was one of the best times of the month in Thea's opinion. Kaylee was not only a fantastic artist, but she also used her studio and warehouse to host individual art lessons, as well as nighttime theme events such as Brushes With Lushes.

Kaylee was up at the front of the room, demonstrating the next technique so they could draw their flower and moonscape, while the rest of the class looked on with wine and paint, ready to go.

In other words, Thea got to play with paint, work with a theme, have some wine, and hang out with her best girls. Her sisters surrounded her, while Abby sat on the other side of Roxie, her teeth biting into her lip as she concentrated. Thea had invited Molly once again, but the other woman hadn't been able to make it. At this point, Thea wasn't sure

Molly was *ever* going to come to a night of Brushes With Lushes, but Thea would feel bad if she didn't ask.

"Stop feeling guilty about Molly," Adrienne said from her right.

Thea paused with her paintbrush in the air. "Huh?"

"You're thinking that you feel bad that Molly isn't here, and you're blaming yourself for once again locking lips with Dimitri."

"Shh!" Thea whispered, looking around to see if anyone had heard them. Their group was in the back row since Kaylee knew they were usually the loud ones. The Montgomerys and their crew couldn't help it, they didn't get out much.

"Don't shush me when I'm right." Adrienne set her paintbrush down and sighed. "I'm not reading your mind, you just whispered her name as you were grumbling to yourself. Molly has never once come to this with us. It's not her thing. That's fine. She doesn't need to hang out in a huge group with us. But I want you to ask yourself if you're feeling guilty because you feel like you need to or because you really do."

"You're smiling when you think of him, babe," Roxie said softly from her other side. "I haven't seen you smile about a man in far too long."

"Smiling is good," Abby put in, leaning over Roxie. "And you said yourself, Molly is okay with you seeing Dimitri."

"It's just all too weird." Thea took a sip of her single glass of wine, wondering once again how she'd gotten into this situation. "And I should stop telling you every time I kiss

Dimitri because I *told* myself yesterday that I wasn't going to tell the world about what I was doing and then two minutes into seeing all of you again, I blurted everything."

Adrienne reached out and patted her knee. "Of course, you did. I sucked at hiding what I was doing with Mace and hated not telling you all everything. So don't hold back. We promise not to harass Dimitri." She paused. "Much."

"In other words, we're happy for you," Roxie added. "Dimitri is hot. Sweet. And according to you, wickedly amazing in bed." Her sister thankfully whispered that last part.

Abby leaned over again. "So why aren't you out with him tonight?"

Thea sighed. "Because I already had plans with you guys. It's Friday night, and it's what we do. Dimitri and I have a tentative dinner planned for tomorrow night, depending on the bakery and his time with Captain. And I know that sounds cheesy or weird that I'm scheduling my time around a dog, but I love Captain, and I hate that they don't get much time together thanks to Dimitri's housing situation. With Captain getting on in years, I'm not going to stand in his way." She frowned. "And if one of you says *I'm* getting on in years, I will personally slap you. Hard."

"Since I'm older than you, I'm going to refrain," Adrienne said dryly.

Thea turned to Roxie, whose eyes were dancing above the rim of her wine glass. "Oh, don't worry. I won't say a thing."

"Can we get back to painting? Because I'm behind a step I think, and Kaylee's going to yell at us again."

"I won't yell, but how about I say I'm disappointed."

Thea jumped as she turned to see Kaylee standing behind her, shaking her head, but there was a smile playing on her lips, so it couldn't be too bad. "Don't fool around too much." Then Kaylee flowed across the room, her skirts billowing around her. Thea always admired the other woman's style and the graceful way she moved.

Thea was pretty sure she still had flour on herself somewhere. It was always on her. Lying in wait for someone to happen upon her and comment on it.

"Let's focus for a bit, shall we? Then you guys can make fun of my social life or lack thereof."

Roxie snorted "Since we're with you this evening for girls' night, I'm not going to mock you for your lack of social life. We *are* your current nightlife."

Thea laughed while focusing on Kaylee as the other woman explained once again how to complete the next step. Thea decorated cakes often, but she wasn't the best painter in the world. Adrienne was better, but as her sister was a tattoo artist, it made sense. Roxie tried her best, but wasn't the greatest at it either, not that any of them commented on it. Their little sister was so methodical and *had* to get everything right that she usually got in her own way.

As that was basically a metaphor for Roxie's life outside of Brushes With Lushes, Thea couldn't help but think of how Roxie and Carter were doing. Every time Thea saw her sister, she looked a little more...worn. Or perhaps the thin armor she wore against the world wasn't quite as shiny as it used to be. Thea wished she could help her sister and brother-in-law, but she honestly had no idea what was going on between the two. Besides, she knew it wasn't her business, even though her family always wanted to know about *her* life. And not just her sisters, her brother and parents were just as bad.

The only person missing from their painting night was her sister-in-law Shea, who was home with Livvy and Shep for the evening. If she were here, Thea knew Shea would be peppering all of them with questions so Shep knew what was going on with his baby sisters. Thea never minded because Shep asked things himself when he was around, and since he wasn't invited to Brushes With Lushes, he sent Shea instead, who was amazing and could get anything out of anyone at any time. It was sweetly diabolical, and Thea was so damned glad Shea was a Montgomery.

"What do you have planned this weekend?" Abby asked the group.

"Work?" Roxie answered though it sounded like more of a question. "I'm actually not sure. Carter and I wanted to go see a new movie, but I'm behind on a new filing thanks to a client and things I can't talk about, so I might send Carter off to the shop so he can get ahead and maybe we can have Sunday afternoon off or something."

Thea held back her wince. The two were constantly working, and Thea knew that Carter was doing his best to hire on more people and budget well so he could spend more time with his new wife, but Roxie's job didn't make it easy. Putting together two lives and trying to make it work was hard, hence why Thea had never really tried.

With her business perhaps changing soon if things came together, she knew she might not have time for a love life, and dating might go by the wayside once again. That was another reason why she was questioning herself about things when it came to Dimitri.

The others spoke around her, and when Adrienne mentioned Mace and the guys having wings, Thea pulled herself back into the conversation.

"We're thinking of going on a family road trip once spring hits and the mountains are a little more passible. Daisy loves the little hikes we go on, and if Mace and I schedule just right, we can take a couple weeks off."

"That won't put the shop in a lurch without the two of you?" Thea asked.

"Not really. Ryan and Shep can handle most of it, and Mace and I will just make sure we have that time free booking-wise. And if it looks like we need another artist, one of the ones from Denver can come down. When Austin and Maya helped us open this branch down here, they knew it was part of the deal, as did the rest of their artists. It'll work out."

Adrienne shrugged, her attention on her painting. "We can't do a super long trip like we might want to, and frankly, I don't know if Daisy is up to that anyway, but a long weekend would be nice. I know we live in the mountains, but there's so much more to see."

Thea smiled, she couldn't help it. Her sister had always been in Daisy's life, if only on the periphery. When Daisy had been living with her mother, and Mace hadn't had the best custody agreement, Adrienne was still always there. Thea was so happy that the new little family was making it work in their own way, and Adrienne was taking to the role of almost stepmother perfectly.

"You look so happy," Roxie said softly from Thea's other side. Soft, but loud enough that Adrienne heard. "You deserve to be happy."

Adrienne leaned over Thea and patted Roxie's arm. "I *am* happy. Thanks, babe. And you're shading that with the wrong grey, want some help?"

Roxie frowned and looked at her canvas while Thea held back a grin. "It's fine. Right? Why does this have to be so hard? I mean, why are there so many colors?"

Adrienne shook her head and went around Thea so she could stand behind Roxie. "Why are there so many numbers and ways to make accounts?"

"Math makes sense. Painting, not so much." Roxie bit her lip, and Thea set down her brush so she could turn to her sisters and mediate if needed. Both were perfectionists but in different ways and, sometimes, that difference got under each other's skin. It was the same for Thea, but they were sisters, and that was just life. Abby looked on, a smile on her face as she set her brush down, as well. The two of them toasted each other with their glasses in the air and watched as Adrienne tried to help Roxie with some of the moonscape, and Roxie tried not to get frustrated when she didn't get it right.

It might have been Brushes With Lushes and just a fun night, but Roxie wanted to learn how to do it better, and of the four siblings, she was the one who had trouble coloring in the lines because she got impatient with not being able to do it correctly the first time. Thea didn't mind getting a little messy, but that was why she was a baker and not a tattoo artist like two of her siblings. She was also decent at math and business—hence the changes coming up with Colorado Icing—but Roxie was her accountant for a reason. And the fact that Shep's wife, Shea was also an accountant helped. Between the two of them, Thea knew she was in good hands.

Of course, as soon as she thought of good hands, she thought of Dimitri. She took another sip of her wine, trying *not* to think of him.

How was this going to work? She'd thought maybe they could try to be friends, but now she was worried that she'd screwed everything up by kissing him again, by wanting more from him. It scared her.

Because she liked him. A lot. She liked being near him, liked kissing him, and she sure as hell more than liked their night together. Yes, it was all far too complicated, and there were so many ties and strings tightening around what they could be that it was almost suffocating, but she didn't know if walking away was the right answer.

Molly was okay with it.

Dimitri seemed to be okay with it.

Thea, deep down, was okay with it.

Maybe she needed to trust that part of herself.

Maybe.

"When are you going to come in and let me work on your shoulder again?" Adrienne asked when she went back to her seat. Roxie was working on her wine rather than her painting, so Thea figured the two had finished their little mini-lesson while she was lost in her own thoughts. Considering that neither of them was covered in paint and there hadn't been yelling, Thea counted it as a win.

"Huh?" Thea asked, blinking away the cobwebs from her brain.

"Your shoulder. The tattoo you wanted." Adrienne said. Her sister tilted her head, studying Thea's face. "You okay over there?"

"I'm fine. Maybe I've had too much wine." She set her almost-empty glass next to her easel and shook her head to clear it.

"You haven't even finished your first glass, but okay. Anyway, what about that tattoo? It's my turn on you since Shep got your hip last time when we first opened the shop. When can I have you?"

The two were always fighting over family members and their ink. It was the same for their Denver cousins, and Thea didn't mind it. The Montgomerys were the best in the business, and she counted herself lucky that she'd always have some of the most amazing ink out there and would never, ever have a bad tattoo anywhere on her body.

"When I have time, I guess. Or rather, when *you* have time. Your shop is bustling over there, and I know you have massive waitlists already, which is awesome. I don't want to push anyone out of the way so you can work on my shoulder. Plus, the fact that I *need* my shoulder and arm to work makes the idea of all that soreness not so much fun. And it's not like I have time for a vacation in order to make it work."

"First, you work too hard, but we can come back to that. Second, you're adorable in thinking I wouldn't have space open for you or a walk-in monthly. While I need and love heavy schedules, I'm also an artist who sometimes needs to do things out of the box or completely random. That's where you come in."

"I want flowers and characters from my favorite movie on my shoulder, not something random," she said dryly.

Adrienne rolled her eyes. "The random is for the walk-ins, dork. Not that I'd pick a random tattoo for them, but it's random for *me*. As in, I don't have it planned in my head for months but they know what they want, and it keeps my creativity going. You know? As for you, though, we can do the pieces in shifts so we don't make you too sore. I know you want it on your right shoulder, and since that's your dominant side, it'll be tricky with how much you whisk and stir and use that arm to do things, but it's not like it incapacitates you. Plus, you don't swell as bad as some people, and you follow directions when it comes to aftercare. We can make it work."

"I know we can, but I probably won't have time until after...well, until after the season." Yes, she was busy during the holiday season, but she also had her new plans coming up that she hadn't explained to the others yet. She knew she needed to tell them soon since they not only owned their parts of the building, but because they were family. Roxie knew but had kept her mouth shut. The only reason her little sister knew at all was because she was Thea's accountant.

Thea would tell Shep and Adrienne her news soon, but for now, she was a little worried and a little scared that it wouldn't all work out. Change was hard, and making plans for something crazy like what she had planned was even harder.

Adrienne gave her a look but didn't ask any questions, and for that, Thea was grateful. Kaylee made her way around the class again, commenting on their paintings, and Thea went back to it, trying her best to get it to look like Kaylee's. Of course, it wasn't perfect, and she'd taken some artistic license when it came to the moon, but she loved it in the end. After the class was over, the whole group got up to take a photo with their paintings, and Thea left hers to dry with the others, knowing she'd either come back to pick it up for her house or Kaylee would find a good use for it. There were tons of people around who wanted art but couldn't afford it, and yeah, it wasn't the best work in the world, but she was happy to know that at least two of her paintings were in shelters for women and children. It wasn't much, but maybe it could make someone happy.

"Are you ready to head home, or do you want to hit a bar

or something?" Adrienne asked as they pulled on their coats.

"I need to head home since I promised the babysitter I'd be back by eight," Abby answered. "Sorry."

"You know Mace said you could bring her over to hang out with Daisy if you want," Adrienne said as she wrapped her scarf around her neck. "He's already at home, you know? That way, you can stay out as long as you want and not have to worry about a sitter."

"Mace would be the sitter then, and I'd still pay him, even if he said he wouldn't take the money," Abby put in.

"Think about it, at least," Adrienne said. "Or know that if you can't get a babysitter, one of us is here."

"Heck, our parents would love it, too. They try to get as much time with Daisy and Livvy as possible. They love babies." Thea grinned as she said it. "I think they're waiting for the rest of us to have more kids, but now that Mace and Daisy are in the picture, it takes the pressure off of us."

Roxie coughed. Thea couldn't tell what was wrong with her sister, but she noticed that the other woman had gone pale.

"Everything okay?" Thea asked.

"Oh, yeah, I'm fine. I could do with a drink. Carter is at home, but I know he had a few piles of paperwork to get through. So maybe if I'm home by nine, that'll give him enough time, and then we can have the rest of the night together."

"A drink sounds good to me," Thea said. It wasn't like she had someone waiting at home for her. She wasn't going to call or text Dimitri, no matter how much she wanted to. Instead, she was going to talk to him tomorrow and possibly see him for a date. Nothing too scary or momentous.

And if she kept telling herself that, she'd totally believe it.

THEY SAID their goodbyes to Abby and headed over to the bar next door to Kaylee's studio. Kaylee herself couldn't make it since she had a later event but told them all to have fun as they strolled to the other building. Soft guitar music drifted out of the open door, and Thea glanced at the sign next to it on the sidewalk claiming it was open mic night.

"This could either be amazing or horrible," Adrienne said under her breath as Roxie laughed.

But Thea didn't laugh, she couldn't, not when she heard that voice.

She *knew* that voice, dreamed of that voice. Oh, hell, that voice was one that kept her awake at night and sent delicious warmth between her thighs.

"Is that...?" Adrienne's voice trailed off, and Roxie sucked in a breath.

Thea just blinked as they stopped right inside the door, the three of them standing stock-still, their mouths dropping open.

Dimitri sat on a stool in front of the crowded room, his fingers strumming the guitar as he crooned a song about love and loss with that deep growl of his.

And when he lifted his head, and his gaze met hers, he didn't pause, didn't break his concentration, but she knew he saw her, understood that he wanted her there from the glint in his eyes. Realized that this meant something.

And she knew...she *knew* she was lost.

And so damn screwed.

CHAPTER 13

*D*imitri wasn't sure how he kept playing when he saw her there, but he made his fingers move, made the song come from somewhere deep inside him, and just *sang*. When he got to the end, he closed his eyes, putting everything he could into the lyrics, then let out a breath. The room went silent.

He opened his eyes as the cheers and applause began and smiled at the crowd, thanked them for their time, then packed up his guitar. Some called out for another set, but his turn was over, and he knew damn well he wouldn't be able to sing with Thea in the room.

He didn't think she'd known he was there, and wasn't sure she even knew he sang at all since it hadn't been something he did often in recent years. Molly hadn't been a fan of his music since she liked pop tunes and classical, and that wasn't something he was interested in. Plus, going to dive bars for open mic night had *really* never been her thing, so he'd quit doing it. He'd had too much on his plate with work and going to all of Molly's functions, that playing for himself like this had gone by the wayside.

Like so many things he liked to do.

He'd willingly given them all up because he'd thought he loved Molly enough to make it all worth it. But it hadn't been until he was on the outside looking in that he realized how *much* he'd given up when Molly hadn't done the same for him.

Dimitri didn't want to think about that, however, because Molly wasn't here. She was his past, not his present, and sure as hell wasn't his future.

The woman staring at him like she hadn't seen anything like him before, however...*she* was someone he wanted more of in his life. The fact that she stood between her sisters, all of them looking comically surprised at what they'd just witnessed, made it even better.

He made his way around the crowd as the next person got ready on stage. He liked Tamsin, the singer who came on after him, and she had a bigger following than he'd ever had—or would. That meant the crowd would be focused on her, and Dimitri could focus on a certain Montgomery.

"Hey there," Adrienne said with a rough laugh. "You pulled a Giles there, didn't you, Dimitri?"

Roxie started giggling at the reference, but Dimitri only had eyes for Thea. "Giles?"

"From *Buffy*," Thea explained, her voice hoarse.

"That show with the vampires?"

"Yeah," Adrienne answered. "Some of the crew goes looking for Giles, and they find him playing music like you were just now, and he's all hot and growly and totally surprises all of them."

Dimitri finally looked at Adrienne, shaking his head. "Hot and growly?"

"Well, yeah," Roxie put in. "I mean, it was the first time I noticed him as the hot guy with the broad shoulders and that deep British accent. Before then, he was the staid librarian that aided Buffy during all the apocalypses. He was never a hot guy. You know?"

Thea rubbed her hand over her face, and he noticed the flecks of dry paint on her skin. The three of them must have been at their Brushes With Lushes night and had evidently just finished. Now that he thought about it, Kaylee's studio was nearby, so them coming in tonight made sense.

Still, though, he couldn't keep his eyes off Thea, and from the way the other women were giving each other looks, he knew he wasn't being anywhere close to subtle about it.

"So...Giles?" he asked softly.

"Giles." Thea licked her lips, and Dimitri did his best not to think about that tongue and where he wanted it.

"You know what? I'm going to head home and see how Mace is doing," Adrienne said quickly.

"Oh, yeah, Carter probably misses me." Roxie bounced away, waving over her shoulder, and Adrienne practically skipped behind her, leaving Dimitri alone with Thea.

The fact that Thea hadn't said much, but the two of them

were still standing in the middle of the walkway staring at each other spoke volumes. He needed his coat, needed to get the rest of his things before he headed out of this place, but he could only think about the woman in front of him and how much he wanted her...how much he needed her.

And not just for sex.

It was never just about sex when it came to Thea Montgomery.

He realized he wanted to know what she thought about him up there, how she felt about his little hobby that he hid and kept to himself. She might have said the word *Giles*, but what exactly did she mean by that? Did she like it? And why the hell was he just standing there thinking stupid things and not pulling her close for a sweet way to say hello?

"You...you play guitar?" she asked, blinking quickly. "How did I not know you play guitar?"

He reached out and ran his knuckle down her jaw, unable to stop from touching her any longer.

"I guess there are a lot of things we don't know about each other." He paused. "But I'd like to figure them out. What do you say?"

She shook her head, and his heart deflated until she took a step closer, put her hand on his chest, went on her toes, and brushed her lips against his.

"I think my teenage self is remembering *exactly* how I felt when I saw Giles all hot and growly, and I think you should come to my place because I *really* want to kiss you again. What do *you* say?"

He let out a breath and forced himself not to adjust his

rigid cock straining the zipper of his jeans. He might end up with teeth marks there—and not from Thea—but it would be worth it for this moment alone.

"Giles does it for you, then?"

"The Giles effect is an enigma and a fantasy for many." She smiled as she said it, and he kissed her hard before tugging on her hand.

"I need my coat, and then I can follow you to your place. You okay to drive? I know there was probably wine at your paint thing."

"I'll be okay," she squeezed his hand as they walked. "I didn't even finish my first and only glass since we were all talking and painting and everything that comes with a night with the Montgomery girls and Abby."

"Abby came?" Dimitri asked as he pulled on his coat from the back room. "I'm glad. I don't know her all that well, but she's really nice when I stop by her tea shop."

"She's great, and I'm glad she's getting out more, you know?" Thea rocked from foot to foot. "It is weird that I just asked you to my place? Shouldn't we do our date tomorrow like we talked about and just...I don't know...part ways tonight?"

She practically whispered the last part, and he held back a curse. He didn't want her to feel like she was doing something wrong or that they were rushing, but he also didn't want them to second guess every part of whatever this was between them because they were worried about all the ties that bound them together.

He set down his guitar case next to them, ignoring the others milling about, and leaned down to cup her face.

"We don't have to do anything you don't want to do. All you mentioned was kissing thanks to the Giles effect or whatever the hell you called it. Remind me to watch *Buffy* with you at some point so I can actually understand the reference."

Her lips quirked in a smile, exactly like he'd intended.

"I know we had plans for a tentative date tomorrow thanks to Captain and my grading, and we can still do that. Or we can take the time we have now if you still want to and maybe have a drink at your place. I only say your place because you're not only most comfortable there and you suggested it, but it's also bigger than my shoebox apartment that still smells like the old tenant."

She leaned into his hand, and he smiled, loving the way she didn't shy from his touch in public—or anywhere for that matter. They were still so new to this, still trying to figure out what they were to each other and how they could make it work—whatever *it* was—but this was a step. It had to be.

"I guess we can do a mini-date tonight. I have to work tomorrow, and one of my staff thought she might have to stay home tomorrow anyway if her kid doesn't get over his cold. Babysitter issues or something. That means I'll have to work a double on Saturday. Which is fine, but it's not the easiest thing. If that's the case, I'd have to cancel anyway."

"That sucks that your staff member's kid is sick. But you're a good boss in that you understand."

"I have to be. I trust my people with my dreams and livelihood, and that means they need to be able to rely on me, as well. But that *also* means while I try to schedule breaks for myself, sometimes I don't get to choose when I work. I have to be everything, you know? But Colorado Icing is my baby, and I'm okay with that."

He kissed her temple, then leaned down to pick up his guitar. "I get it. I put my students before almost everything in my life except maybe Captain. Most of my weekends are spent on lesson plans and grading and learning the new program the state dumped on us last-minute. The only reason I'm out tonight is that I know I'll spend all day tomorrow working on all that paperwork since Molly is taking Captain to some event."

He rolled his eyes as he said it, and Thea blinked. "An event. With Captain?"

"Don't get me started. But it's some charity for a local shelter, and Captain will get love and attention, so I guess that's okay. One of her fellow board members, Hoxton—yes, that's his real name—is actually really good with Captain and will probably spend the whole day with him while Molly does whatever she does best and earns money for the committee. So, I'm okay with it. It just sucks."

"I know. And I still hate that you don't have much time with him." She frowned. "Would it be weird if you hung out at my house sometime with him? That way, you can work if you need to, but you're still with him? I don't know how Molly would feel about that, but it's not like it's your fault the apartment doesn't allow pets."

He could have fallen to his knees right then in gratitude that she would even offer that. And when he said as much, she snorted.

"It's for Captain. Not you. I love that dog."

He thought it was a little bit about him, too, but he didn't say so. "I love that dog, too. And I might just take you up on the offer since hiking is getting hard with all the snow storms we've been getting, and it's only going to get worse after the new year."

"Then let's see if it works out." She paused. "That's what friends are for, right?"

He played with the ends of her dark hair. "And if I want to be more than friends?"

She looked up at him, so much emotion in her eyes, he could only understand a fraction of it, though he had a feeling they mirrored his own. "We can be both. Friends and...friends with what we're trying. Right?"

He leaned down and touched his lips to hers, a bare whisper of what was to come, of what could be. "Right?"

And he had a feeling that no matter what happened between them, this friendship would be exactly what he needed.

What they needed.

No matter what.

CHAPTER 14

*D*imitri sucked in a breath as Thea licked up and down his neck. This wasn't like the first time, and it probably wouldn't be like the next time. First, because there was *going* to be a damn next time. Secondly, because he'd already had a taste.

Now, he'd get his next helping.

Then again.

And again.

And again.

"Who knew playing guitar could do this?" He pressed Thea against the front door, and she shivered.

"I didn't know I had a kink. It's a damn sexy one."

"Kink away." He bit down on her shoulder, then paused, leaning back to look her in the eyes. "Just don't call me Giles when I'm inside you and you come on my cock."

She snorted, leaning her head against his shoulder.

"Yeah, not so much. Now get naked with me, because I need you. Now. Don't make me call you Giles."

He grinned, then went back to licking her neck. When her fingernails dug into his back, he groaned, the sharp sensation in his skin sending shivers of pleasure down his spine. Then he slid his hand between them and under the waistband of her jeans over her panties. She sucked in a breath, and as he pressed a bit firmer against her heat, cupping her, she arched into him.

He wanted her. Craved her. And now he was going to have her.

"You're already wet for me." He couldn't move around too much without taking off her pants, but he wanted to tease, wanted to make her squirm. "I'm not even inside you yet." *Pat.* "How wet are you going to be after my mouth is on you?" *Pat.* "Are you going to drip down my chin? *Pat.* "Are you going to let me fuck you hard tonight, Thea?" *Pat.*

"I'm always wet around you it seems. That's the problem." She licked her lips, and his dick twitched.

He was just able to trace his middle finger along the swollen edge of her lower lips. "You're swollen. Wet. And ready for me. And I need to taste you."

"You will. I want that head between my legs, but first…" She wiggled away from him, and he removed his hand.

"First?"

"I need your dick. I've had this dream where I'm on my knees, and we're both dressed but I'm taking you right to the edge. Can I play?"

He swallowed hard, and without answering, undid his

belt. When she grinned and went to her knees, he couldn't help but think of every sweaty dream he'd had of her recently. Her on her knees in front of him was better than any fantasy.

And when she pulled his cock free and licked the tip, he knew *she* was better than a dream. He ran his hands through her hair, closing his eyes when she licked up the vein on the underside before hollowing her cheeks to bob along the tip. His balls tingled, and his dick stiffened even more when her tongue slid along the slit at the tip.

"I need to come inside your pussy, not your mouth. Not tonight." He tugged at her hair, and she leaned back, her eyes filled with triumph.

"I'm going to swallow, you know. Because I want to. Just saying."

He grinned then lifted her up so she stood in front of him and he could kiss her. He wrapped her hair around his fist, tilted her head to the side, and took her mouth.

"We can do that. But first, I need to fuck you. Tuck my cock back inside, Thea."

She met his gaze at the order—and yeah, it was an order—before doing just as he asked. When her breath caught, he knew she liked it.

"I'll let you order me around this time, Dimitri. Just this once."

He reached around and gripped her ass, picking her up. Her legs went around his waist, the heat of her core scorching against his straining dick.

"You can order me next time."

"Promise?" She licked her lips.

And because it was an invitation, he leaned over and bit down on her lower lip. Hard. "Promise."

He carried her to the bedroom, and after he'd set her down, he stood back and slowly stripped off his shirt.

"Take off your pants, shoes, and panties. Leave your shirt on." He winked as he said it, stripping off his shoes, jeans, and boxers so he was completely naked.

She raised a brow. "Got a problem with my boobs?"

He licked his lips. "I have plans for your boobs."

She rolled her eyes but did as he asked, and before she could comment, he had his mouth on hers as he tugged on the bottom of her shirt. She lifted her arms, and he had it over her head but didn't completely strip it from her arms.

"What are you doing?"

"You'll see."

Then he walked her back to the bed and slowly laid her down, her arms above her head, tied up in her shirt. He lay between her spread legs, willing himself not to touch her below the waist and make them both lose their minds, not when he wanted to pay special attention to her breasts.

"Oh, I see." She laughed, then let out a groan when he sucked on her nipple through her bra. He reached around her back, undid the clasp, then pushed the whole thing up so he could see all of her.

"You look so fucking beautiful."

"You're not too bad yourself. If you angle just right, your cock can slide right in." She didn't move her hips, though. He wasn't wearing a condom yet and was being *very* careful where he touched her. They weren't at the part of their relationship where he could go bare. They were still in the beginning stages, no matter how it felt when he was near her.

He licked and sucked on her nipples until they were dark red, and she squirmed beneath him. And when he wanted to touch her, when he wanted to slide deep inside her, he bit down gently, using his fingers to delve between her legs. Heat radiated from her as he slid one, then a second finger into her, stretching her as he worked his way inside. And when she came, he had his mouth on hers and had to think about anything but what she felt like beneath him so he wouldn't come.

She blinked up at him, her eyes dark, her pupils wide as she struggled to catch her breath. As he was the same way and he hadn't come yet, he didn't blame her.

"Condoms are in the drawer."

He kissed her, then left her where she was, her hands above her head, her bra askew...looking glorious. He quickly went to her nightstand and opened the drawer, only to find himself grinning.

Dimitri slid the condom over his length, but when he went back to her on the bed, he wasn't empty-handed.

Her eyes widened. "Um...Dimitri?"

"I've never seen a vibrator like this." He grinned. It was small, fit perfectly in his hand, and had a nozzle-like opening at the top. "What does it do?"

She swallowed hard, and his gaze went to the long lines

of her throat. The fact that she hadn't moved her arms made his balls tighten.

"It blows little puffs of air on my clit. Like when someone goes down on me."

"Like I would when I go down on you."

She nodded. "Yeah. But Dimitri, I need you inside of me. I...I'll come really hard with that and I'll be a mess."

He leaned beside her, his hand and the vibrator going between her legs. "Let's see, shall we? You tell me to stop, and I will."

"Don't stop." Her mouth parted, and he pressed the on switch. It wasn't as loud as other vibrators or even his cock ring, and it took him a moment to figure out exactly the best place to place it over her clit, but he knew from the way her breath quickened and her nipples hardened, that he'd found the sweet spot.

Again.

This time, when she came, she shouted his name, her legs clamping around his hand. He quickly turned off the vibrator after moving, then positioned himself between her legs, sliding into her with one thrust.

Her inner walls were still shuddering, and when he was inside her to the hilt, they both groaned.

"Dimitri."

He leaned forward, took her lips, and quickly undid her shirt and bra so she was free to touch him all over. And when she did, he pistoned in and out of her, his mouth on hers, his hands on her body. Her hands roamed as well, and when his balls tightened again, he took her mouth and came. Her body shook beneath his, and she clamped down around him.

He shook with her, and soon they were holding one another, their bodies still connected, and he knew from this moment on, nothing would be the same.

She was his.

And now he had to figure out what to do about it.

What they *could* do about it.

CHAPTER 15

hea knew she shouldn't be nervous, but she couldn't help the butterflies flitting around inside her stomach. This wasn't the first time she'd given this presentation—not that it was an actual presentation—but it was the first time she was going to tell her parents exactly what her next plans were.

Plans that didn't center around finding a husband or having children. Her parents had never been the type to push her in that direction, but there was always a kernel of worry that they'd be disappointed she was once again focusing on her business.

She knew it was the right decision, knew this was the path she needed to take. And as she remembered Dimitri's hands and mouth on her the two nights before, she knew that she wasn't *only* focusing on Colorado Icing anymore.

And though she and Dimitri were new and not thinking

about what could happen next, at least she wasn't locking herself up at her bakery anymore, ignoring everything else around her. She'd done that for years while trying to keep herself in the black, and that was how she'd ended up far lonelier than she'd ever thought to be at her age.

But she had her business, had her way of life that she loved—long hours and all—and damn it, she wasn't so far along in years that marriage and babies were out of her grasp. She needed to get a grip and stop overthinking everything. This was just what she did when she was nervous, however.

And telling her parents about the expansion sure as heck made her anxious.

"Oh, boy," she whispered under her breath, rolling her shoulders back as she did so. Her parents were pulling up, and it was time to seal the deal and actually let herself be a little excited about her future. Excitement and nerves usually went hand in hand when it came to Colorado Icing.

It was a Monday afternoon, and her staff was working at the counter and in back, so Thea could have a needed break. It wasn't that busy, only a couple of customers staying in to eat as the bakery was between major rushes for the day, so this was the perfect time to sit with her parents in the back corner where they could easily have a conversation without worrying about being overheard. She could have done this at either of their homes or in the back office, but she wanted to tell them her news while they were surrounded by what she'd built as they stood by and supported her with every ounce of love and hope they had.

William and Katherine Montgomery were two of the best people Thea knew, and she loved them so damn much. She knew she was lucky in terms of parents, and though her mom sometimes wanted to try and fix everything in her kids' lives, she also stood back and let them make their own mistakes and revel in their triumphs. It was something Thea had always appreciated, and now that she was old enough to understand it, she was glad that she could recognize the traits in them.

Outside, the clouds loomed overhead, and the forecast called for snow later in the day, but only a dusting, something every person from Colorado could easily handle. She winced at those thoughts since that wasn't exactly true after seeing so many people end up in fender-benders because they weren't paying attention, but with the predicted dusting, her bakery should pick up business for hot drinks, and her staff would still be able to make it home at a reasonable hour. Since she'd opened, she wasn't going to close, but she'd stay late in case one of her people needed to head home early for their kids. That was Thea's job as their boss, and so far, none of them had taken advantage of her.

She stood up as her parents walked into the bakery, unwrapping their scarves and pulling off their hats.

"Mom, Dad, thanks so much for coming." She opened her arms and brought each in for a hug, squeezing them tightly because, sometimes, she just needed her mom and dad.

"Of course, we came. You wanted to talk, and I heard there would be cookies and perhaps cupcakes." Her dad winked, and Thea moved to the side, gesturing for them to sit at the table she'd set up for them.

"Let's see, I have carrot cupcakes, peanut butter cookies, pecan and almond bars, fruit salad, and some of my new onion and white cheddar rye rolls." She grinned as her dad licked his lips, and her mom let out a little laugh.

"I think I just gained forty pounds looking at all of that," her mom said before leaning over to kiss Thea on the cheek. "Thanks for the fruit so I don't feel guilty when I try everything."

"That's why the fruit's there."

Her dad just shook his head and took the spot nearest the window after pulling out the chair with the back to the front door for Mom. Thea took the last seat so she could face the bakery if there were issues, and she loved the fact that her dad knew that she needed that place without her having to say anything.

Before she took her seat, however, she wrung her hands together, trying to keep the nerves at bay.

"What can I get you guys to drink with all your goodies today?"

"You're spoiling us," Dad said before taking a bite of one of the rye rolls. "And if this roll isn't on your menu from now on, I'll never forgive you."

Thea couldn't help but grin. "Yeah? Oh, yay, I loved it, but they're all powerful flavors, and I wasn't sure if it would be too much."

Dad shook his head before sipping at the water she'd put on the table ahead of time. "It's perfect, not overpowering in the slightest. And once I'm through with this one, I'm heading into sweet territory, so how about just plain black coffee? I know I'm adventurous with food, but you know me and coffee."

Thea couldn't help but laugh. "I know. I should have just brought you a cup without asking, but I didn't want to tempt fate. Mom? What about you?"

Her mom looked at her for a moment, and Thea had a feeling she wasn't hiding her nerves all that wall.

"Do you have some of that lovely tea Abby has over in her shop? The peppermint and white chocolate one?"

Thea grinned. "I do, and I think I'm going to want some of that today, as well. Be right back." She quickly made her way around the counter and began steeping the loose-leaf tea, as well as pouring her dad his cup of coffee. They had five kinds of beans today, but her dad would want the most average one she had. Things hadn't changed in twenty years, and they wouldn't start today. That was okay, though, because her dad was her best taste-tester for her baked goods.

By the time she carried all three drinks to the table—thankfully, something years in food service had trained her to do without spilling—her nerves weren't dancing as much as they had been before, but as soon as she sat down, they started again in full force.

She tried to think of how to start as her parents dug into the sweets, something they rarely did at home since Thea usually brought the baked goods seeing as it was her passion.

"Why don't you tell us what's in those files you have hidden in your bag next to your chair? The ones that you've been glancing at ever since we got here as if you're afraid someone will walk out of here with them." Her mom reached out and patted her hand, and Thea's shoulders relaxed. She hadn't even realized she'd stiffened as much as she had until her mother's touch.

"I can do that," she said, then reached down to pull out her paperwork. She set everything down on the space she'd cleared away from the drinks and food. Of course, these were only copies so if they were spilled on, it wouldn't be a big deal. She didn't leave the important paperwork near her kitchen or anywhere they could pick up mass amounts of coffee stains. She'd learned that lesson the hard way when she first started.

"What is it, hon?" her dad asked, setting down his coffee. "Are you okay?"

She nodded, swallowing hard. "I'm okay. Healthy and everything."

"Is it about Dimitri?" her mother asked, and Thea froze. "Uh…"

"My friend Kathleen saw you two at a bar a couple of nights ago and told me. I wasn't going to say anything since I figured you'd mention it when and if you were ready."

Thea ran a hand over her face. "No, the paperwork doesn't have to do with Dimitri. And I'm not going to talk about him right now. Okay? And what could these papers possibly have to do with him anyway?"

Her mom blushed, shrugging. "I don't know. It seemed

like a good way to mention that I know, though, since I hated not telling you."

"There's nothing for me to tell."

Her mom raised a brow.

"Fine, there's nothing to talk about right *now* when it comes to him. Can I talk about what's in this folder, or should I just go and bake some more?"

"Talk about the folder, though I do love your baking," her dad put in.

Thea let out a breath. "As you know, the bakery is doing well."

All three of them immediately knocked on the wooden tabletop, and Thea let out a laugh. Superstitions were part of her life, even with little things like knocking on wood and spilling salt.

"Anyway," she paused, chuckling again. "The business is going well to the point where I've been saving up for what to do next. I mean, with Colorado Icing that is. I've been saving for other things too that don't have to do with the bakery, but for now, I'm...well..." She shook her head. "Sorry, I had a whole speech planned out in my head, and now I can't remember it."

"We're so proud of you and Colorado Icing," her dad said quietly. "You started with a dream, and you've kicked butt. Plus, you let me taste everything, so I'm happy. Well, happy other than the fact I have to work out more to compensate, but it's worth it."

Thea just smiled. "I love you guys."

"We love you, too," her mom said. "Now spill, Thea. You're killing us here."

"The place next door is going up for sale soon, and the owner is willing to sell to me before she puts it on the market. It's been empty for a little while now while she gets her next place ready, and I really feel like I can make this happen. As it is, there's not enough seating during rush times, and the kitchen isn't set up for a full lunch. Right now, I do a few sandwiches, but I want to do more. I want to make sure people come to us for our drinks and baked goods, but also for lunch and other needs. I'm making it work now and even offer a lot of that already, but I want it to be a little more streamlined, I want more room. And I know I can do it. I'd have to hire on a person to help me handle it all at least part-time, but that would be part of the loan and startup costs to merge the two parts of the main building. It would be a lot of work, but I'm ready. Roxie thinks I can get the loan, and if I have the right paperwork with the right references outside of family, I really think this could happen."

Thea bit her lip as she stared at her parents, worried that they'd say something like this was too much or that she needed to take a step back and think of her personal life.

She shouldn't have worried.

They were Montgomerys, after all.

Her father immediately stood up and went to hug her tight, her mom coming around the other side, doing the same.

"This is going to be amazing, and I'm so damn proud of you. I can't wait to see what happens," her father said.

"You're going to kick ass," her mother said, and Thea laughed. "What? I curse all the time."

"I know, I just love when you do."

"Are you going to get your Denver cousins to do the renovation? Or what about the Gallagher brothers up in Denver? I know they do restorations, but since one of the brothers married into the Montgomerys, they'd work, too."

Thea rolled her eyes. "I was already planning on calling the cousins if things work out with the loan. I don't want to put too much pressure on myself or them if it all falls apart. But I should mention that a qualification for being good at your job shouldn't just be that you're a Montgomery or related to one."

Her dad scoffed. "Ha. How little you know."

"Honey, she knows a whole lot if she's going to take this on. I know it's a lot of work, but I also know you've already thought it through. Your dad and I might be retired, but we're also here if you need us. Don't do everything on your own if you can't. I'm not talking about money," she added quickly when Thea opened her mouth to protest just that. "I'm talking time, labor, and anything else you need from us. We love you, Thea. You're our baby girl even though you're all grown up."

Thea blinked away tears and hugged her parents hard. "I love you guys. I was so worried, and I know I shouldn't have been."

"Damn right," her dad said with a wink before taking his seat again once Mom did.

"Now, tell us everything," her mom said. "We want to hear it all, and you'd better eat a few of these carrot cupcakes with me because I think I just fell in love with this frosting."

Thea laughed and took a big bite, relief spreading through her even as the anxiousness of the paperwork and what was to come warred inside.

By the time her parents headed out, and Thea went back to the table to clean up and put away her paperwork—she'd kept an eye on the table the whole time so no one could come around and snoop—she was a little tired and very full but happier than she had been in ages about the potential developments. Her parents believed in her, they always had, and having them at her back meant the world. Soon, she'd tell the rest of her family her plans, but this hurdle was a big one.

She was just stuffing her papers back into her bag when Molly walked in, pulling off her big glasses.

"Thea, darling, oh good, you're here. I'm dying for something sweet, and since I can't even *look* at cake like you do, I need hot fruit tea. Anything sugarless you have." She kissed Thea's cheek before Thea could even get a word in. "Oh, what's all this?" she tugged the last piece of paper out of Thea's hands and read a few words. "Loan paperwork? Oh, no, are you in trouble?"

Thea winced. "Shh, Molly. No, we're not in trouble. This is for something else. Everything's fine."

"Are you sure? Because you know I can help if you need it. Daddy can, too."

Thea wanted to crawl into a closet and hide away from this conversation, but she might as well get over it. The fact that this was just one of many awkward conversations she'd had with Molly recently made her worry, but she didn't have time for that kind of anxiety, not yet anyway.

She tugged on her friend's arm and pulled Molly toward the office along with her paperwork. The bakery was filling up, and she didn't want to have this conversation where everyone could hear. It had been different with her parents and the time of the day.

"What is it? Why are you tugging me? Do you need money?"

"I'm *fine*," Thea repeated. "This is loan paperwork for an expansion. You know the empty part of the strip on the other side of me? Well, I want to buy it and make Colorado Icing into something even bigger."

Molly's eyes widened, and she clapped, her smile going into something so fierce that Thea took a step back. "Oh, that's wonderful. Loan paperwork needs references, right? I never needed a loan since I've always been able to just use the money I have, but I've heard that."

Thea held back from saying something not quite nice since Molly had money only because of her parents, but speaking about it wasn't going to help anyone right then.

"Yes, loan paperwork needs references."

"Let me be your reference," Molly put in. "I've known

you forever, and with my family name and connections it should be a breeze."

And though that fact grated on Thea slightly since Molly hadn't ever worked a paying job, what her friend said was absolutely true. Plus, the idea that Molly would so readily offer without Thea even having to ask was sweet.

"That would be amazing."

"Yay! I'm so glad I can help. You know, if I cared about baking and could be near sugar, I'd totally buy the place next to you, and we could be partners."

Thea blinked, wondering how the hell Molly had come to that realization since doing that would change everything and not work out in the slightest, but she assumed her friend must be joking. Surely.

"Ah. That would be...interesting."

"But I run from sugar as most sane people do," Molly said with a wink. "Just let me know what I need to do for the reference, and you have me. Now, I really need that tea before I get my nails done. Snow's coming, and I can't deal with that and wet nails."

Thea just shook her head, lost as usual at Molly's erratic train of thought. She walked out to the front with her friend and froze.

Dimitri stood at the counter, coffee in hand. He looked between the two and gave them a strained smile. Yes, this was awkward, yes, this was complicated, but damn it, Thea was happy to see him.

Even if Molly being there made things dramatically weird.

"Oh, hey there," Molly said with a grin. "Seems we're thinking the same thing. Tea for me. What did you get?"

"Hazelnut latte." Dimitri cleared his throat. "Hi there, Molly. Thea. I'm headed out to a workshop but wanted something hot to drink. Late night with paperwork."

"Same for me, probably," Thea said as she moved to stand behind the counter to work on Molly's drink. "Exciting, right?"

"You know it is. Anyway, I need to head out. Thanks for the drink. Have a good rest of your day, ladies."

Thea knew it would have been too awkward for him to hug her, to kiss her, to do anything that stated who they were to each other when they didn't know that for themselves yet. Doing anything in front of Molly would have just been weird and perhaps even mean to the other woman, so they were walking on eggshells and trying to figure it all out.

Slowly.

Thea watched as Dimitri walked out, and Molly leaned forward to pat Thea's hand.

"Watching you two makes me so happy. I know it's weird, I know I shouldn't want it, but if you like each other, then keep going for it. I just want my two best people happy."

Thea cleared her throat. "We've...we've been on a couple dates." One real one, but they'd been together twice, though Thea would *not* have that conversation again.

"Love it!" Molly took the tea from Thea's hand and stopped bouncing. "Oh, make sure you make him shrimp linguini one day. It's his favorite, and I never was able to make it. I'm not a cook, and raw shrimp makes me want to run away in terror."

"Oh, I don't know…"

"Do it. We're trying to make this work, right? Make sure our friendship stays intact as you try this new avenue? Well, I'm just trying to help. He'll love it. Trust me. Now, I have to leave, but don't forget the linguini!"

She sauntered out of the shop, pulling on her big glasses again while Thea stood back and wondered how this had become her life.

Times had changed, and yet part of her hadn't, and she wasn't sure what to make of it all.

CHAPTER 16

*D*imitri cupped himself at the base of his cock, groaning into the shower stream as he thought of Thea on her knees in front of him, those juicy lips wrapped around his length. He flexed his hips into his fist, licking his lips as he tightened his grip.

He imagined her sucking on the tip of his dick, licking up the drop of fluid as she hollowed her cheeks around him. She'd flick her tongue over him, hum along his length as she cupped his balls in her hand, giving him a squeeze that would make his eyes cross. Then she'd reach around and play with his prostate just like he liked so he could fuck her mouth with care even as they were both lost to each other.

Then, when she was done with him, he'd move to her, lick up every inch of her as he played with her nipples, her hips, her ass. Every. Damn. Inch.

And when she looked into his eyes, they'd both come

together, their bodies shaking, sweaty, and pressed so tightly against one another, they'd remain that way until they could breathe again.

"Thea," he whispered, his body shaking as he came hard, his seed jetting from him, hitting the tile wall in front of him and sliding down into the water below. The water had cooled, and his arms ached from how long he'd been doing this that morning.

Coming three times at the thought of Thea because he couldn't get his mind and dick off her probably wasn't the healthiest thing in the world, but it was either that or go to her house later with such a hard-on that he couldn't focus.

And he wanted to focus.

He wanted to get to know her even more, be part of her life even when they weren't having sex. He just wanted her.

And they were slowly on their way to that point in their relationship when their wants and needs were being met, and they were finding out who they were together rather than just apart. It should be scary, should have made him worry more than he was, but he was…happy.

Because of Thea.

And now he was cold, aching, and spent because of thoughts of her.

Jesus, he needed to get a grip.

And not just on his dick.

He snorted, finished washing up in the cold water—the colder, the better according to his libido—and dried himself off while thinking of the rest of his evening. He'd worked all day, and had come home to work out rather than grading since his brain couldn't focus on paperwork that night. As soon as he got dressed, he'd head over to his old place and pick up Captain. Thea had wanted him to bring Captain over for dinner, and he was happy that she was taking them both in, thrilled at knowing how much Thea loved his dog. That meant, however, that he'd have to see Molly tonight, but things were getting better between the two of them. They would never be friends like they had been, but they could be cordial. Plus, she was friends with Thea, and that meant Molly would be there if Dimitri wanted to be in Thea's life.

He'd find a way to make it work. He had to. After all, he'd been the one to pursue Thea, the one who urged her to be with him, so he was the one who would try his best not to mess everything up when it came to her and the relationship they had with each other and the one she had with Molly.

Yeah, starting something new with a different person might have been ten times easier, but it wouldn't have been *right*. He liked Thea. He...cared about her. More than he thought he would after everything that had happened. He'd always liked her, though, just not the same way he did at this moment.

When he was married, he hadn't looked at Thea in the same way he did now. Thea had always been there, was always his friend and in his life, but things were different these days.

Things were...better.

And now he had to wonder what would happen next.

Because the two of them were still finding their balance, still figuring out who they were to each other. They were friends, and they were...more. They weren't good with labels and, frankly, he wasn't sure they needed them. At least not yet. They were finding their way, and in doing so, they were having fun. He never wanted to hurt Thea, but he also didn't want to hurt Molly.

He might not love Molly anymore, but he didn't want to throw his new happiness in her face.

Once again, he knew it was all too complicated, but he wasn't going to walk away.

Not yet.

Not when there were still sparks between him and Thea. Not when his feelings were growing by leaps and bounds every time he was near her. He wasn't good with words, wasn't good with owning up to his own emotions, but he was learning.

For Thea.

He cleared his throat and grabbed the rest of his things so he could head over to pick up Captain before going to Thea's. He wasn't sure what he was going to tell Molly, if anything. It wasn't her business where he went, but Thea might have mentioned it already. He wouldn't lie, but he also wouldn't offer up any information unless Molly outright asked. He didn't want to make things harder for any of them.

By the time he made it to his old house, he was coming to his own revelations. He missed his dog, but he didn't miss much about his life here. He hadn't really liked this home, hadn't really felt like it was his if he were honest. It had been Molly's. It had made her happy, so he'd been happy for her.

The only part of his old life he missed was his dog, and now he could take Captain with him for a couple of hours. He didn't think that Thea was replacing part of what he'd had, but more making her own place in his life. He hoped he was doing the same for her.

Molly was at the front door again before he knocked. She had Captain by her side, and his bag of treats, food, and other needs in hand.

"Have fun tonight," she said with a wink. "I know Thea will take care of you. I'm seriously so happy for you two."

He gave her a nod, still confused about her enthusiasm regarding his relationship with Thea. He didn't know why Molly seemed to want this so much, but it seemed to him that he and Thea were the only ones feeling like there was something off.

Off wasn't the right word, but the two of them were walking on eggshells to make sure they didn't hurt Molly. And the thing was, she didn't look hurt. She didn't act hurt. Hell, she seemed happy.

And maybe it was time for the uneasiness to stop.

"Thanks," Dimitri said as he went to his knees to pet his dog. "I'll be back later with him since he can't spend the night with me."

"I'm sure he can spend the night at Thea's with you." She grinned as she said it, and something uncomfortable settled over him.

This was weird…right?

Or maybe he was the one making it weird.

"I don't know if that'll work tonight." He wasn't going to say that he didn't know if he and Thea were ready for that. What went on between the two of them was only for them. Yes, Thea might tell Molly some, but he didn't think either of them wanted to reveal every part of their lives together and apart. He'd have to talk to Thea about it, though, because honesty between them was essential.

"Oh, you never know. Have fun and make good choices." Molly laughed as she said the line from one of her favorite movies and he gave her a nod before taking Captain and walking back to his car.

"Weird," he mumbled under his breath. The whole situation was weird. The only time it didn't feel that way was when he was with Thea. That's how he knew he was doing the right thing, even if everything on the periphery seemed off. He hoped that it would settle down around them soon because he didn't want the outside world harming what he had—and what he *could* have —with Thea.

Dimitri buckled Captain into his harness, then headed to Thea's. It didn't take them long to get there, and the closer he got to her place, the more relaxed he became. Yeah, there was some anticipation there—there always was when it came to Thea—but he was just happy that he got to see her soon.

And while his dick ached at the thought of her, he wanted to spend time with her, wanted to know more about what went on during her day. Texting at night and phone calls when they couldn't see each other was nice, but he wanted more.

He paused after he'd parked.

He wanted more.

Hell...well, then.

Apparently, he wanted more.

Captain whined behind him, and he quickly shut off the car and got out to unhook Captain. Thea had her door open and grinned as Captain bounded over to her. She went to her knees and rubbed his dog down, laughing as Captain licked her face and whined to get even closer.

"Hey, buddy. Let her breathe." Dimitri grabbed his bag as well as Captain's, shaking his head as he shut the car door and made his way to the pair.

"I can breathe just fine. I missed this puppy so much. Who's a good boy? You're a good boy. Yes, you are. Yes, you are." She singsonged the words, and Dimitri couldn't help the wide smile covering his face.

"You're going to spoil him."

She got to her feet, brushing away some of the dog hair from her pants. She wasn't going to get it all, and he loved that she just shrugged when she noticed that fact.

"Maybe. I also maybe have an s-n-a-c-k in the kitchen for him. Maybe."

He shook the bag he had in his hand. "I have some, too. And thank you for spelling it. Though from the light in his eyes, Captain might know how to spell that word now."

She just winked and leaned down to kiss the top of Captain's head. "Our boy is pretty smart."

He knew she'd only said *our* because she loved Captain too, but a small part of him paused at the word, liking it far more than he should this early in their relationship. He was still finding out who he was without his marriage surrounding him and yet...and yet.

"Come on in, I didn't mean to make you guys stand out in the cold. We'll get Captain settled, and I'll go back to making dinner."

"Sounds like a plan." He moved closer to her as she stepped back to let Captain in and kissed her softly on the lips. "Hi, Thea."

Her cheeks blushed, and she smiled. "Hi, Dimitri."

"Thanks for having us."

"I missed Captain." He kissed her again. "And you, I guess."

"I guess," he teased and walked into the house. The place smelled of herbs and warm food, and his stomach growled at it all. "Smells wonderful."

She smiled at him, but there was something in her eyes he didn't understand.

"What?"

"I had planned on something else for tonight, but Molly said this was your favorite and I decided to make it instead. I got it in my head that she was so excited about it, and if it's your favorite...well. Yeah, probably not the best idea, but we're going with it."

He shrugged. "Thea, baby, we're figuring this out together." He set the bags down on the floor while Captain roamed. Then he cupped her face, kissing her softly. "This isn't a normal relationship for either of us. She's your friend, and I see her more often than not because of Captain. She's part of our lives, and that means we need to be respectful and also find our own path. I get that it's weird as hell, and not everyone will understand, but we'll make it work."

"I want to make it work. And that means making concessions and knowing things are odd but not letting that be the only thing that matters." She moved forward and was the one to kiss him this time. "Now, enough about that, let's have some wine while dinner warms on the stove."

"Wine sounds good. But first…" He cupped her face again and kissed her, needing her taste, craving her taste. She moaned into him, and he arched into her, loving the way she bit down on his lip when they parted.

"I love your kisses," she murmured.

"You kiss pretty fucking good, Thea. I think I'm addicted."

She grinned wide. "Good. My plan is working."

He kissed her some more, all of his attention on her as his hands roamed over her. He wanted her naked and beneath him but remembered his promise. Tonight was about getting to know her, not more, not right then.

"This was a pretty damn nice way to start the night." He kissed her temple, and she sighed.

"I'd say. How about that wine?"

"Sounds good to me. Let me set out Captain's things. The fact that he's lying in front of the fireplace already and getting comfortable makes me happy."

"He makes me happy because you're happy." She shrugged as she said it and went to get the wine. He watched her walk for a moment, then went to take care of his dog.

"So, what have you been up to other than what you've been texting?" she asked as she made her way into the living room with two glasses of white wine.

"Grading. Seriously. That's it right now at this time of year."

"I'm so glad I'm out of school," she said with a laugh, handing over his glass. "Sorry."

"It's not for everyone. I'm just glad I get your cookies. And cakes. And coffee. I'm pretty selfish." They clinked glasses, and each took a sip. It was a nice, smooth Riesling, and he was happy.

"We work then."

He hoped so.

"What have you been up to?"

"Well...I've been doing my usual things that you know about, but I've also been working on a side project."

He leaned forward. "Oh?"

She swallowed hard.

"What is it?"

"I'm thinking of expanding." She explained her plans, and Dimitri couldn't help but smile. She sounded so excited about it, even as he could tell she was nervous.

"You're going to fucking rock at it. I can't wait."

"It means if it happens, I'll have even less time than I do now."

He shrugged, though that part sucked. "We'll make it work. I'm so proud of you."

"It's scary, but I'm getting excited. And speaking of food and cooking, I need to finish." She left him to head back into the kitchen, and he couldn't help but watch the way she walked.

He liked the way she moved.

"What are we having for dinner tonight?" he asked as they walked into the kitchen.

She stood in front of the stove, blocking his view. "Close your eyes and guess."

He grinned and did so, opening his mouth as she put the fork between his lips. As the first taste burst on his tongue, he knew he'd made a mistake.

He quickly stepped back and opened his eyes, letting out a curse. "Shrimp linguini?"

Her face fell. "Is it too salty?"

He shook his head and pulled out his wallet, reaching for that little pink allergy pill that he used every once in a while. He quickly went to the counter, spit out the pasta in a paper towel and downed his allergy pill. Thea was there with a glass of water without saying a word, and he chugged it, meeting her eyes for the first time.

She had tears running down her cheeks but wasn't making a sound. Instead, she just looked at him with a pale face and wide eyes.

When he finished the water, he leaned against the counter and sighed. "So...I guess I should have mentioned I have a shellfish allergy."

She wiped her face, then went to the sink and washed her hands. "I washed my hands before you came over, and I haven't touched the shrimp since, but I want to be doubly sure. Do we need to take you to the hospital? Do you have an Epi-pen?"

"I'm okay. Really. I don't have an Epi-pen because insurance doesn't cover it and it's way too expensive on its own. Yeah, it's a risk, but I'm usually more careful."

She wrapped her arms around her waist and let out a breath. "I know food allergies. I deal with them carefully at the bakery, but I honestly didn't think of it at home."

"It's not your fault." He went to her, wrapping his arms around her. "My allergy isn't as bad as some people's. And I'm not even a little tingly from it. I'll be fine. I'll get sleepy thanks to the allergy pill, but I'm no worse for wear."

"I'm so sorry. I must have gotten it wrong from Molly somehow."

He frowned. "Maybe. It doesn't matter. No harm. No foul."

"I can't believe I almost killed you."

"You didn't almost kill me. I should have checked before I tasted. I know better. I've lived with this allergy my whole life."

"And yet I almost killed you the first time I wanted to make what I thought was your favorite meal. I should have stuck with lasagna."

"Next time, we'll make that together, baby. I'm okay. It happens. One day, I'll tell you about the time my brother

Devin thought he bought fake crab and ended up making full crab cakes I gobbled down. Mom wasn't exactly happy."

"I don't know how I haven't met your siblings yet."

"It never worked out for dinners at the old place. One day, you can meet Devin, Caleb, and Amelia."

"If I don't kill you with shrimp first." She rested her forehead on his chest, her head coming up under his chin as he held her close.

"It wasn't your fault," he repeated. "My allergy never came up because we live in Colorado and it's not like shellfish is on everything out here. Now if we were on the east coast? Then that's all you'd hear from me every time I walked outside."

"Yay for being inland then." Her tone was so dry that he squeezed her hard. "Thea."

"I'm going to pout a bit since I almost killed you." Captain moved his way between them, and she petted the dog's head even as she burrowed into Dimitri. "Why don't you two go sit on the couch and rest since I know you're going to get even more tired soon. I'll clean up, and I guess we'll figure something out for dinner."

"I can't drive for a bit with the antihistamines in my system, so why don't I order us some Chinese food. I can help clean up a bit, too."

She shook her head as she took a step back. "Nope, you're not touching a thing in here just in case shrimp is out to get you. Thank God I didn't eat a piece or taste test before you came over because all that kissing earlier might have taken a horrible turn." She let out a watery breath, and he hugged her tightly again.

"I'm fine," he repeated.

"You will be. I'm just so sorry I misunderstood Molly."

He wasn't sure she had, and that worried him. Maybe he was just overthinking things. Maybe Molly had it wrong since they'd never had shrimp at the house. She preferred it out of the house in a cocktail. He didn't say anything though because he wasn't sure his brain was firing on all cylinders at the moment.

Molly wouldn't have sabotaged their night, so she must have gotten it wrong. Must not have known Dimitri's preferences and not remembered the allergy. That was one reason they weren't married anymore. But he didn't want to worry Thea, so he didn't say anything. Instead, he hugged her close, breathed her in, and knew they'd make the most of their night.

Because he was falling for Thea Montgomery.

And he wasn't sure what he could do about it and keep them both from getting hurt.

CHAPTER 17

*M*ontgomery family dinners were always an event in Thea's mind, and tonight was no exception. Not only was the whole immediate family and their significant others showing up, but Thea's parents had also invited Abby and her daughter, Julia. Ryan from the tattoo shop, and Landon, Mace's and Carter's friend, would also be there.

Kaylee couldn't make it because of a private art lesson, but she'd said she would send along a bottle of wine with Abby.

And, of course, Dimitri was coming because Thea's mom hadn't taken no for an answer. Not that Dimitri would have said no, but Thea had wanted to save him from the interrogation.

Though there would likely still be an interrogation.

Thea let out a breath, trying not to make it look as if she

were freaking out. Because she *was* freaking out. She'd brought boyfriends to her family dinners before. Her parents were great at making the gatherings larger with the addition of friends of the family like tonight when it came to introducing new relationships. It probably would have been even more nerve-racking if it had just been Montgomerys and Dimitri. Thea had been in a situation like this before, but this was different.

Dimitri was different.

Of course, he was different.

He was hers. *Hers.*

Dimitri reached over and squeezed her knee, his eyes on the road as they made their way to her parents'. "I thought I was supposed to be the nervous one here. Are you okay, babe?"

Thea looked over at him and crossed her eyes. He must have seen her out of the corner of his eye because he snorted.

"I know your parents. And your sisters. And the rest of them. In fact, I just hung out with the guys minus Shep and your father the other night. Shep has done one of my tattoos, and Adrienne's trying to get at my other arm. They know me."

"They know Dimitri Carr, friend of Thea. They don't know Dimitri, the guy I'm seeing."

"At least you didn't say the guy you're doing."

She growled at him, and he laughed. Laughed. "This isn't funny. I'm bringing a man home to my family. And *everyone* will be there. I'm stressing out."

He squeezed her knee again. "I know. I'm not as calm as I'm trying to appear, but we're not teenagers or even in our twenties anymore. I've been married before, Thea."

"That's part of the problem," she muttered.

They stopped at a red light, and he looked over at her, frowning. "With you? Or with your parents."

"I don't know." She blew out a hard breath. "And I don't actually think it is a problem. It's more the fact that they already know so much about our history, so I'm afraid they're going to skip the normal interrogations and go right for the hard stuff."

The light turned green, and they started moving again. "And there's going to be a ton of people there with their own issues. I'll take what they dish out. It's okay. Plus, I've done game night with most of them, so this is just a new part of what we're doing together."

"Game night was before we started seeing each other."

Dimitri looked over at her as he parked behind Shep's SUV. "If I remember correctly, game night was when it all started."

She could feel her cheeks heat. "Let's not mention Twister." She paused. "Though I should say that uh…my sisters and the girls know exactly what went on."

He coughed as he shut off the car. "Like…all the details?"

Thea grinned, giving him a wink. "Pretty much. It's what we do. I know *lots* of details about Mace."

"Jesus," he said with a laugh. "And what about Carter?"

She paused. "Not as much, but then again, Roxie is pretty private when it comes to him. I know she's the only one of us girls married, but she likes to keep him to herself."

"I get that, honestly. Sometimes, you need that. I take it Shea doesn't tell you everything about Shep?"

"Not so much since we stop her before she gets to details."

"Yeah, I know a few things about my siblings' love lives, but not all the details. I don't know what I'd do if I had to hear details about my baby sister."

His baby sister was almost as old as Thea, but she didn't mention that.

"Let's get inside," she said after a moment. "Because if we don't, they'll just come out here anyway and press their noses to the windows like Captain does."

"So many nose marks."

They made their way to the Montgomery front door, Dimitri holding their cheese plate—because, of course, they brought cheese—and Thea holding two bottles of wine. She knew others would bring beer, but she was seriously in need of wine tonight.

Her mom opened the door as soon as they rang the doorbell and grinned. "Finally! The others are already here. Now the party and torment can start." Her mom's eyes went wide, and she mock gasped. "I mean, party and tea. Yes, a tea party. Not a torment party. No torture here."

Dimitri just grinned and leaned down to kiss Thea's mom's cheek. "I hope I can handle a little torture, Mrs. Montgomery. I've been preparing."

"Call me Katherine. There're so many Montgomerys here that it just gets confusing."

"Okay, Katherine. I can do that."

"And you brought cheese. I figured Thea would bring her amazing plate, so I didn't make one myself. I used to make a damn fine charcuterie plate, and then Thea came along, and I had to step up my game."

Thea just rolled her eyes. "I have high cheese standards. I didn't bring dessert, though since Abby wanted to bring some, so I'm scaling myself back."

"I thought you could use a break," Abby said as she walked into the room, a toddler with big eyes in her arms, sitting on her hip. Thea loved little Julia, though she didn't know her all that well. Yet.

Julia blinked up at Dimitri and held out her arms, surprising all of them. Abby let out a laugh and shook her head.

"No, baby girl, let Dimitri settle first before you tackle him. She likes big men." Abby blushed.

Thea laughed. "She has good taste."

"I'll say. If you help me with the cheese, Katherine, I'll take this little star."

Her mom took the plate from Dimitri, and he held out his arms. Julia went right to him, and he bounced her a bit in his hold.

Thea knew she wanted children, though she hadn't known how much until she saw Dimitri holding Julia. Could she feel her ovaries? Because she was pretty sure one just burst as her womb pulsated.

Dimitri holding a baby was a thing of dreams, and as she caught her mother's knowing look, she knew she was in trouble.

Deep trouble.

"Let's get you inside with the rest of the crew," her mom said after a moment, her gaze darting between Dimitri and Thea. "We have wine open and beer in the smaller fridge."

"Sounds good to me," Dimitri said with a grin before blowing a raspberry on Julia's cheek.

Yep, there went her last ovary. Boom. Just like that.

Her mom led the way, Abby following while looking over her shoulder to check on Julia. She'd tried to take her daughter back from Dimitri, but the little girl clung to his neck, and Dimitri waved her off. Thea didn't blame Julia one bit as she clung to him as well, and when Dimitri met her eyes, she had a feeling he knew exactly what she was thinking.

Thea soon found herself with a glass of wine in hand, trying to follow Dmitri's progress throughout the room. Ryan stood next to her, snorting over his beer every time Dimitri was pulled into another Montgomery embrace. Thea had wanted to be by his side, but her mother had nixed that idea without a word. Apparently, Dimitri was going to the belly of the beast unaided.

"I need to save him," she whispered under her breath.

"He's fine," Ryan said on a laugh. "Isn't this how the meeting of the parents usually goes?"

Thea glared at him. "First, Dimitri has met everyone in

this room before. Secondly, it's not usually like a procession where I'm pushed away from helping."

Ryan just shrugged before taking a sip of his beer. "That was the old Dimitri. This is the new one. Go save him."

"He doesn't need to be saved." She bit her lip. "I don't think. But maybe I should go just in case."

"I would. Montgomerys are territorial. Or so I hear."

She raised her brow. "Date a Montgomery in the past I don't know about?"

"Uh, no, but I work with two, so I see how you guys are. Not that I have a problem with that since you have each other's backs. Now, go save your boy."

Thea rolled her eyes but went to Dimitri's side anyway. Somehow, she slid between him and her mother, wiggling under his arm so she could be by his side and save him from more interrogations.

Her mom just laughed, shaking her head. "We weren't going to eat him alive, Thea."

Her dad let out a rough chuckle. "That comes after dinner. You know our schedule."

"I seem to remember a dressing down when they thought Adrienne wasn't watching," Mace added when he walked up to them, Adrienne by his side.

"And I was totally watching, but I figured he deserved it since he'd annoyed me that morning."

Thea snorted, and Dimitri put an arm around her shoulders, giving her a quick squeeze.

"When do the pliers and duct tape come out?" Shep

asked, grinning. His wife Shea elbowed him in the gut, and he winced. "What was that for?"

"Your parents were nothing but nice to me when I first met them. I mean, really, I was just some girl from New Orleans with RBF, aka resting bitch face. I'm surprised I was even allowed to take the name Montgomery." Shea grinned as she said it, and her husband leaned down to kiss the tip of her nose.

"You've classed up the Montgomerys, babe."

"I'd take offense to that, but it's true," Roxie added dryly. Carter stood behind her, not touching her but close enough that Thea figured he wanted to reach out and hold his wife. Only they were both so stiff that Thea thought maybe she was just projecting.

Thea liked Carter, she really did, but as the days went by, he and her sister didn't look happy, and that made Thea want to cry for them. She wished Roxie would just talk to her, damn it. Talk to any of them. But no matter how hard they tried, how much space they give her, Roxie never opened up.

Dimitri squeezed Thea again, and she looked up at him, hoping her emotions weren't on her face. The others were talking about Shea's move to Colorado with Shep and their daughter, but Dimitri's eyes were on her.

She smiled, knowing that it didn't reach her eyes, but she tried to push down her worry. She might be the second to youngest and still close in age to both of her sisters, but she always looked out for her baby sister.

And she'd never felt so helpless.

"And then there was that time with the cupcakes," Shep was saying.

"I know how to bake," Shea complained. "I had pregnancy brain. Being pregnant with all those hormones during tax time did not lead to good baking. I mean, who knew I'd mix up salt and sugar. It could happen to anyone."

Thea grinned. "I've done that once."

Everyone looked at her, wide-eyed. "Seriously?" Landon asked, standing between Ryan and Abby. She didn't know him all that well, but he was part of the family now since the Montgomerys tended to adopt friends.

"What?" she asked, her smile real this time. "It was once, I was tired, something was mislabeled. I was young, what can I say?"

"It takes all kinds," Shea said, shaking her head. "No one ate it, right?"

"No, I caught it in time. What about yours?"

Shea looked over at her husband and smiled wide. "What do you say, baby?"

Shep winced. "I didn't want to make her feel bad. It was…interesting."

"True love," Ryan said after they all stopped laughing. "It makes you do interesting things."

Thea wondered if Ryan had ever been in love and realized that she didn't know much about him. She didn't know much about many of the people in her sibling's lives. She'd spent so much time working on her business, and was about to put even more into it, that she'd lost sight of others. She leaned into Dimitri's side as the others talked, with the two older kids running around them, laughing. Abby's daughter had fallen asleep soon after Dimitri had held her since it was past her nap time. Thea took in all of it, realizing that if the loan paperwork went through, she would have to put more effort into finding a balance between work and life. She'd thought she was doing pretty well, but now that she looked around, she knew that she hadn't done as good of a job as she could have.

The fact that she was here with a man, someone she cared about who she could easily see herself falling for was a step in the right direction.

She just hoped she didn't ruin it all once things got busy again. She didn't know how she'd juggle everything, but she'd try.

She had to.

CHAPTER 18

*B*y the time dinner was over and they headed back to Thea's house, she had a headache but wasn't down for the count yet.

"You did so well with them."

Dimitri grinned at her as he set down his keys next to hers. She tried not to get a weird feeling about that, how well his things looked next to hers, but she couldn't help thinking about what would come next—and not just for that night.

"Really?" he asked. "Because I was sweating there for a few minutes when your dad sipped his wine and stared at me over the glass. He didn't ask what my intentions were with you, but he was damn close with the whole plans and school thing."

Thea winced. "Sorry about that. At least you had an answer."

They both went to her couch, taking seats next to each other so they were touching but still able to speak to one another easily.

"An answer I'm not that happy with. The whole administration there is changing, and it's making it hard for me to work without showing my ink. You know?"

She traced her fingers down the dark trees on his forearm. She'd always loved that ink, and it was a shame that he had to hide it during the day when he hadn't had to before.

"Maybe things will change."

"I'm not quitting. The kids need me and, frankly, I need them." He cupped her face. "And I don't want to move to a different school district. If I did, well, I'd have to move away from those I care about."

She swallowed hard. "Like Captain."

He smiled softly. "If I left, I'd take him with me. If I had to go, though, I wouldn't be able to take you with me. Your life is here. Your family. Your work. You've put your heart into it, your life, and I can't take that away from you."

Her heart raced. "I can't be the only reason you're staying, Dimitri. I can't handle that pressure."

His thumb traced her cheek. "I'd never do that to you. That's my roundabout way of telling you that you're important to me and that I care about you. That I want to keep doing what we're doing and seeing who we can be together." He leaned forward and kissed her lips so softly that it was barely a whisper. "You're important to me, Thea. You're... you're so much."

Her heart clutched at the words, and not because he

hadn't said the three most wanted to hear. Neither of them was ready for that kind of declaration yet. The one he'd just made, however, was precisely what she needed, what she'd never thought she could have. Not with him, anyway. It had always been a dream, a far-fetched idea when it came to finding someone she could care about. And then Dimitri had shown up out of nowhere, even though he'd always been there, and her world shifted off its axis.

She leaned forward and kissed him harder, wanting him, needing him, craving him. "I want you in my life, too. This was a big step tonight, and I think you surprised them. You surprised me."

"Oh, yeah?" He bit her lower lip, and she shivered.

"Yeah."

"Let me surprise you more then."

He was on her in a flash, her back on the couch, his body between her legs as he kissed her, exploring her mouth with abandon. Thea touched him, needing him, wanting him. She wanted all of him, and it wasn't fair that there were so many layers between them. Dimitri must have understood because, somehow, they were both naked on the couch in a flash, her pussy over his face, and her face right over his cock.

"How...how did you flip us so easily?" she asked, stroking his rigid length in her palm. "I mean, I'm not complaining, but I still don't know how you got me naked so fast."

He spread her thighs, humming on her pussy. The sensation rocketed through her, and she closed her eyes, taking a few quick breaths to regain her composure. She was such a quick trigger when it came to Dimitri, and they both knew it.

Sure, they both liked it, but she wanted his mouth on her clit for longer than two seconds, and that meant she needed to hold back her orgasm for just a bit longer.

"Babe, you were the one undoing my pants. We're a team when it comes to dual stripping."

He wasn't wrong.

She let out an exaggerated sigh before yelping as he bit her inner thigh. In retaliation, she grazed her teeth along his cock, and he froze.

"That's what I thought." She grinned, then went back to licking down his length. She tried to keep her attention on his dick, on the way he filled her mouth, the way she sucked on his balls. But every time she got into a rhythm she knew he liked by the way he flexed his hips, he'd suck on her clit just right. And because her couch wasn't the widest one in the world, she had to be careful not to relax too much, or they'd both end up on the floor, and no one would be coming.

But then he spread her cheeks and blew on her before biting down on her clit.

She came, hard, squeezing his dick in her hand as she did so. He groaned, and she figured he must have enjoyed it because he lifted his hips into her hold.

"What...did...I...say...about...teeth?" She was having a hard time catching her breath, and when she looked over her shoulder, he just grinned, patting her ass.

"You liked it."

"Maybe."

"No maybe about it."

Then, somehow, she was in his arms, riding him as he slid deep inside her, having put on a condom as the two of them moved into position. With her hands on the back of the couch, it gave Dimitri the perfect opportunity to play with her breasts, and she couldn't help but arch into him, rocking her hips and lowering herself up and down over him.

He filled her so completely, was almost too big for her, though she knew that wasn't quite true. It was just at this angle that it was hard for both of them to concentrate. At least that's what he'd told her.

And this time when she came, he did too, and she knew she'd be lost to this man forever. It wasn't just a game, wasn't just a night with Dimitri. He'd survived dinner with her family, had done everything to make sure she felt as special and cared for as possible.

And she knew if she weren't careful, she'd fall for him.

But if she looked closer, she might realize she already had.

CHAPTER 19

*D*imitri put away the last of his grading, his eyes crossing, but he knew he had a long night ahead of him with a beautiful woman, so he could at least celebrate a bit. Once he entered his grades into the antiquated system his school used, he'd be done for the semester and would have a few days off before the holidays, and then a few days to prep for the next semester. He never truly had a full break, not even during the summer, but that was his job, and he'd learned to love it, long nights and all.

Tonight, however, was about him and Thea and a fancy date at a restaurant with white tablecloths and candles. Neither of them could usually afford the place, but Thea had gone to culinary and pastry school with the chef, and he had invited them for a special tasting during regular dinner hours. Dimitri didn't mind playing fancy for the evening, and he was damn excited to see Thea in a dress.

And then he imagined what he'd do later with that dress and the curves underneath and well...

He let out a groan, adjusting himself behind the fly of his jeans. He really needed to get a grip—and not on his dick.

Having a hard-on at a place where the cost per plate was four times as much as he generally spent on himself for dinner was going to be interesting, but he knew he'd have a good time.

He'd be with Thea, after all.

Dimitri couldn't believe that he'd almost told her he loved her the week before. He'd employed practically every other way to let her know about his feelings, but he'd seen the look in her eyes as he started speaking and knew he needed to take a step back and just live in the moment.

He loved Thea Montgomery.

He had no idea how it had happened or when it had become love over caring and need, but here he was, about to get ready to go on a date with the woman he loved—the woman he couldn't tell that.

Not because he was afraid she'd run, not really. But things had moved really fast for them once they realized who they could be to one another. They had a complicated past that came with more than one kind of baggage. And that meant they had to worry about more than their feelings for each other.

They were standing atop a house of cards where one wrong move could topple it all.

That's why Dimitri was doing his best to make sure they were building a foundation and going slow, even though they were in a precarious position. If they tried hard enough, if they understood who they were and how they could be with one another, they could build their own house made out of something far stronger than cards.

Dimitri frowned, blinking down at his desk. Apparently, he'd been spending too much time with his sister if he was spouting random nonsense about cards and houses and building. Amelia was pretty amazing and way better at emotions than he was—at least he thought so.

"Time to get ready."

He didn't know why he was talking to himself, but he needed to shower and put on some of his best clothes to go out to dinner with the woman he loved. The woman he'd tell that to one day soon. She needed more time, and frankly, so did he.

When she could look at him, be with him, without worrying about hurting his ex, then they'd both be ready for the next step. As it was, he still had a strange feeling when it came to Molly. On the surface, she seemed happy for them, almost pushing them together. Beneath it all, though, he worried that he was missing something. Maybe she was trying too hard, or perhaps he wanted to see something wrong. But he hadn't forgotten the shellfish episode and found he was paying far more attention than he used to when it came to how Molly spoke to Thea. Sometimes, he swore she almost put Thea down as she spoke, but he couldn't be sure.

Molly had always been good at subtle insults and passive-aggressiveness—one reason they were no longer married—but he hadn't noticed her doing it to Thea before now. Maybe she always had, and he just hadn't noticed, or perhaps he was simply too aware now that he was so protective of Thea.

He wasn't sure, but something was off, and he didn't know what he could or would do about it. He'd do everything he could to keep Thea safe, of course, but he also didn't want to take away her ability to protect herself or ruin a friendship because he was seeing things that weren't there.

That meant he had to actually talk to her about it.

That wouldn't be awkward at all.

Dimitri snorted, then went to take a quick shower and get ready for his date. He planned to meet Thea at her place since she had to get ready at her sister's house after a family meeting, and then he was going to spend the night at her house, so he had to pack a bag. He'd already left a toothbrush at her place, but he didn't know if she was ready for him to leave more. One small step at a time, he figured. She didn't spend much time at his place since it was too small for them to have their own space and not be on top of each other—at least when that wasn't the plan. It worked for a single man, not so much for a couple.

That would change, though, he figured. Just how, he didn't quite know yet.

He was just finishing with his tie, his packed bag next to him on the bed when his phone buzzed.

The screen read *Molly,* and he almost didn't answer it, but Captain didn't deserve that.

"Hey, what's up?" he asked.

"I was just seeing if you were going to stop by tonight to see Captain."

He frowned since he'd already told her his plans for the weekend and she'd explained hers, but he repeated it anyway.

"No, I'll be there tomorrow to take him for the weekend. I know you have your event, that way, you don't have to worry about him at your house when you're not home."

"My house. It's so weird to think of it that way."

He pinched the bridge of his nose. "Molly."

"Sorry. Weird day. Anyway, see you tomorrow. Any plans tonight?"

"Just the normal ones," he said, not wanting to get into it. There was something off, and he couldn't quite put his finger on what. Maybe he was reaching, but knew he needed to get Captain out of that house soon so he could finish cutting communication with his ex.

What that meant for Thea and Molly's friendship, he didn't know. But not all boyfriends had to be friends with every person in their girlfriend's life.

"Well, have fun. See you soon, Dimitri."

She hung up before he said anything, and he shook his head, sliding his phone into his pocket. He had no idea what he was going to do when it came to Molly, but he knew it was past time he did *something*. He didn't like the feeling he had these days when he thought of her, and that made him a little sick. It hadn't always been that way, and the fact that he'd chosen her, had thought he loved her, spoke volumes about him rather than who she was now in his opinion.

He pushed those thoughts from his mind, however, and slid on his suit jacket as he gathered the rest of his things.

Tonight, was about him and Thea.

Tomorrow, he'd think about what he had to do.

No matter the cost.

CHAPTER 20

hen Thea met him in the parking lot of the restaurant, Dimitri almost fell to his knees, his breath catching.

"You look fucking phenomenal."

She was in a red dress that went to her knees with a little flair. It had lacy sleeves that ended right below her shoulders, and one of those necklines that made her breasts look so fucking edible, he had a hard time keeping his mind on the rest of her. Her long legs were bare, and he knew she'd be cold if they weren't quick, but he had a few ideas for how to keep her warm. Those shoes, however? Fuck-me heels if he'd ever seen them—black with long spikes. She'd done something smoky with her eyes, her lips matched her dress, and she had her long, black hair in soft waves that tumbled over her shoulder.

He'd always thought she looked sexy and *his* with flour on her face and an apron covering her.

He loved this just as much.

He loved *her*.

She grinned, doing a spin. "You think?"

"I fucking *know*. And if I wasn't worried about putting a hole in one of my two good suits, I'd pray in front of you right now."

"I don't want you to get messy Mr. Sex in a Suit. It snowed earlier, and I'd rather you stay all warm and very hot. Thank you for keeping the beard, by the way."

He ran a hand over his scruff that was a bit longer than scruff. "I know you like it. I trimmed it a bit, though, so I don't look like a ruffian in a suit. I want to look nice for your friend so they don't kick us out."

She went up onto her toes and kissed his cheek. "You look damn edible. I love the fact that *I* know you have ink under all those layers. It's just for me."

He cupped her face. "They're always just for you. Now, let's get inside so you don't freeze, and I don't take you back to one of our cars and take you home."

Her eyes widened, and she laughed. "I forgot. I got blown away by you in a suit."

"Same could be said about you in that dress."

She winked but tightened her long coat around herself so he couldn't see her dress anymore, her sparkly handbag just as bright at her eyes. "Let's go play at being fancy."

"Nothing playing with you in that dress, babe."

"You say the sweetest things." She laughed, and he helped

her navigate the icy patches as they talked about his last days of school and how nervous she was about the loan paperwork for the bakery since she hadn't heard anything back yet. It was just easy. He liked things being easy since they hadn't been in far too long. He just liked being near Thea.

The hostess sat them at a table in the back that was private and looked perfect for their quiet night. When the water came, they explained that their food would be out in stages since it was a tasting, and they were aware of Dimitri's shellfish allergy and had a special menu prepared for the two of them.

"I feel special," he whispered once the waiter left and the sommelier moved toward them.

Thea squeezed his knee. "You *are* special."

He kissed her softly, and she smiled sweetly.

The sommelier gave them a wine list, and both Dimitri and Thea decided to go with whatever wine the restaurant had paired with the meal. That meant a few small glasses of wine and lots of water since they were both driving.

They were on their first glass of wine, a light Pino that made him hungry for something other than the bread at the table, when a familiar voice made him freeze.

"Dimitri? Thea? I never thought I'd see the two of you *here*. What a coincidence."

Dimitri froze, blinking over at Thea, whose eyes had widened before the two of them almost comically turned in unison to see Molly standing in front of their table. She wore a perfectly snug white dress, her long hair pulled up in a fancy twist he'd once known the name for, and she was covered classily in diamonds.

What. The. Hell.

"Molly?" Thea's voice was a bit of a rasp, and Dimitri didn't blame her.

"I love seeing you two on a date at one of my places."

He frowned. "Your place?"

She waved him off. "Oh, you should know. This is one of the places my people come to for dinners with the committee and such. I never thought I'd ever see you two here, but it makes me so happy that I am."

Her people?

And why did she keep saying that she was surprised to see them at *this* place? Sure, they couldn't usually afford it, but her words were getting under his skin. But it wasn't like he could say something right then in public. He didn't want to be the man who hated his ex-wife, but she was making it hard. He was the one who'd chosen her years ago. He was the one who had married her. If he hated her now, that reflected on him and his choices rather than on her in his opinion.

"We're just enjoying our night," he said, knowing there wasn't anything he could say at the moment that wouldn't be awkward.

Thea met his gaze quickly before turning back to Molly. "It's nice to see you, Molly. You look great."

Molly beamed, running her hand down her side. "Oh, I do love this dress. You remember it, don't you, Dimitri?" She winked, and Dimitri barely resisted the urge to growl.

What was up with her tonight? Under the tablecloth, he reached out and gripped Thea's hand, giving it a squeeze. With the way they were sitting, no one would have been able to see the action, and he was grateful. Things were just too freaking awkward already.

Molly continued, "Anyway, I'm off to my table near the bar. Dinner for one is the new me, but you know how I am. I'm fine no matter where I am. I'm sure I'll see a friend soon and join them. I've done it a few times."

Thea looked over at him and winced. Dimitri knew exactly what she was going to say before she said it, and he didn't like it. "How about a drink with us before you go have your dinner?"

Dimitri could only feel like something was off between the women. He didn't know what was going on, but this wasn't the Molly he knew, not the one he'd fallen in love with, and not even the one he'd fallen out of love with.

He was missing something, and yet he couldn't think of what it was.

"I'd love to! Just a drink, though. I don't want to take over your whole night." Molly moved to the side as a waiter showed up out of nowhere to push a chair behind her so she could sit down. She waved him off, and another came to bring her a glass of the same wine Dimitri and Thea were already drinking. He knew the whole thing hadn't been planned, but the show was something else.

Something he didn't know if he liked.

But he didn't like the fact that Molly was having dinner alone, and since Thea was her friend, they'd make do, however weird it was. He just hoped this drink went quickly and he could get on with his date.

Jesus, how the hell had this become his life?

The waiter stopped by and bowed slightly just as Molly and Thea started talking about Molly's day. "We have your first course, a Viennese mushroom in cream, minus the shellfish of course, ready in a few minutes, would you like to wait until your guest is through with her drink?"

"That sounds fine," Dimitri said, clearing his throat. "Sorry for the wait. We appreciate it."

"It's no problem, Mr. Carr. We want to make sure you enjoy your night." With that, the man moved away, and Dimitri looked over at Molly, his memory prickling at something the waiter had said.

Molly winked. "Thank you so much for letting me have a drink with you. I'm almost done, and then I'll let you have your dinner back. Their mushroom in cream is divine, though usually it's topped with delicate lobster flown in fresh each morning since finding lobster in Colorado isn't the easiest."

Dimitri reached out and squeezed Thea's knee. "I'm allergic to lobster, so not having it on the meal works for me."

Molly rolled her eyes. "Of course, you're allergic to shellfish."

"Then why did you tell me to make him something with shrimp?" Thea asked, her voice a bit hollow. There was an undercurrent there that he knew he should be getting, but the thoughts he had of *why* everything had happened didn't line up with the Molly he'd known for so many years.

Molly turned to Thea, her eyes wide. "Did you hear me wrong? I'm so sorry that you didn't understand what I said. I would never want to hurt you guys. Oh, what an unfortunate misunderstanding."

Thea frowned, tapping her finger on the table while Dimitri just stared at Molly, wondering what the fuck was going on.

"Are you both okay? That must have been scary. But I mean, really, Thea, Dimitri's been allergic all his life. I could have sworn we talked about it before."

Thea sighed. "Oh. Well, I guess I just mixed things up."

Dimitri wasn't so sure. He just didn't know why Molly would play around like that. To make Thea feel bad? To hurt him?

Or maybe she was losing herself or her mind...along with him.

Hell, he needed something stronger than wine just then.

"Maybe you did. Wouldn't be the first time, would it?" Molly trilled a laugh. "Now, I must be off, and you should enjoy your date. I see Barney over in the corner. I think I'll see if he wants to join me." She stood up and picked up her sparkly bag that he knew cost more than he made in a month. "Ta-ta, darlings."

Then Molly sauntered off, leaving Thea and Dimitri sitting at their table as if they'd been through a tornado and not a simple drink with his ex-wife and Thea's best friend. A waitress came to take the empty glass away and remove the chair, while another brought their mushroom in cream, minus the lobster.

Dimitri turned to Thea and cupped her face before they started their meal. They were out of everyone's line of vision thanks to their position in the booth, and he needed to know that she was fine, that she was his.

"Hey, want to start the night over?"

Thea gave him a sad smile. "Sure. We can try that. It's just...that was weird."

He nodded, giving her a quick kiss. "Yeah, it was. But how about we try these mushroom things, because I'm starving."

"Sounds good to me."

Only he didn't know if their date would be as good as they wanted to make it. The night hadn't gone as planned, and by the time they'd finished their food, trying their best to act as if Molly hadn't interrupted them and made it seem like either Thea had been wrong or had lied outright about her dinner recommendation, Dimitri didn't know if any of their evening could be salvaged.

They'd tried to do something different, and it hadn't worked. Not even in the slightest.

Dimitri walked Thea to her car after they'd finished dessert, completely full, yet feeling as if he were two steps behind in a game he hadn't known he was playing.

"Is it okay if I just go home tonight? Alone? I have a headache, and I need to breathe a bit." Thea said as she looked up at him, a frown on her face and sadness in her eyes.

He thought about the bag he had in his car, and the weekend he'd planned with her and Captain.

"Okay."

"It's not okay, but…but I think I need to take a step back and remember who I am and why we're doing this. Because something's off, and I don't think it's you. Or me."

He nodded. "Yeah. I get that. Why don't I take Captain up to my brother's house this weekend? We can talk when I get back. Or during. Or whenever. Because I'm not letting you go, Thea. Even if tonight didn't go like we expected."

"I think that might be best."

He kissed her softly, putting everything into it, but he knew this was a step, a moment in time that would become a part of who they were. They would have to find out who they could be together soon, but right then, it was a tipping point.

He watched her walk away, feeling more alone than ever.

He knew something needed to change. There was something wrong with Molly and the way she treated Thea, the way she treated *him*. And that needed to stop.

It had to.

CHAPTER 21

*T*hea pounded her fists into the dough, trying to untangle her thoughts and form the gluten for her bread. There was chemistry involved, baking magic that turned a few ingredients into countless baked goods. But for her, all she wanted to do was put some punch and anger into it. With every fold, every smack of her fist or dough on the counter, she thought that maybe she could get some of this...*oddness* out of her system.

But as she'd been working in the back of Colorado Icing for a few hours now, she didn't know if that would actually happen.

She'd already made loaves of bread, rolls, and two new starters for her sourdough since she was afraid one of her best was starting to lose its action abilities. She'd made cookies, cupcakes, brownies, tarts, and even a mousse for their special today. She'd made frostings, a couple of cakes to order, and had begun baking the tiers for a wedding cake she'd spend the next day decorating with all her energy and creativity.

And she'd done all of it in a fog while trying to figure out what had happened on her date with Dimitri. She hadn't spoken to him since she'd left him standing alone in that parking lot after their uneasy date. They'd texted, or rather, *he'd* texted her, and she responded, just not as quickly and verbosely as she had in the past. He'd gone to Denver to visit his brother and to hang out with this dog, all because she'd needed time to think about what had happened with Molly and what everything would mean to all of them in the future.

"You look like you went ten rounds with the Pillsbury Dough Boy and lost."

Thea's head whipped around at Roxie's voice, her shoulders sagging. All day, she'd been prepared for either Dimitri or Molly to walk through the doors of the café and even come back to the kitchen. All damn day. Neither had shown up yet, though Dimitri had texted saying that he was working at home today on lesson plans, getting a jump start on the new semester. He'd said he'd try to stop by later if she wanted him to.

She'd told him to have a good day.

Why?

Because she couldn't get Molly's weird interactions out of her head, and they were shading her thoughts about Dimitri. She couldn't think when he was around, and the one thing she needed to do was *think*.

"Thea?" Her sister frowned and walked toward her, her arm outstretched. "What's wrong? Do you need to sit down?"

Thea shook her head in answer as well as a way to try and clear her thoughts. "Sorry, I'm fine." She looked down at herself. "Apparently, just covered in flour."

"You're always covered in flour, but when I come and see you during the day, you're not usually trying to take out any anger and aggression you might have on the poor defenseless dough in front of you."

Roxie leaned against one of the cleaner counters and would probably end up with flour on her as well, but Thea knew her sister wouldn't really mind. Sure, her outfit was much nicer than Thea's, and her sister scrimped and saved for them for work, but she also didn't flee from dirt and things.

Unlike Molly.

And that was a thought Thea didn't need to have because she hated that she kept putting the other woman down in her head. Yes, Molly had issues, but they weren't that bad. Right?

The more Thea thought about it, the more she lingered on the digs Molly made, and the way her so-called friend had been acting lately, the more Thea worried that she was only obsessing over it to find fault because she was falling in love with Dimitri.

"Earth to Thea. What the hell is wrong? Don't say you're fine or nothing is wrong. That would be a lie."

I could ask you the same.

But she didn't.

Couldn't.

Thea folded her arms over her chest and leaned against her other counter. "I won't say I'm fine. I was just thinking."

"Want to talk about it?" Roxie tilted her head, studying Thea's face. "Is it Dimitri? Did you two have a fight? Or is it the bakery? I know the expansion sounds like a lot of work, but we've gone through the numbers, if you get that loan with those recommendations, you'll do wonderfully."

Thea shook her head, then rubbed at her temple since the action made that part of her face throb.

"It's not that. Or maybe it's not all of it. There's just been a lot of change happening in a short period of time, and I feel like I'm struggling to catch up. Plus, something just feels hinky, and I have no idea why."

"Hinky?"

"It's a word."

"Well, yeah it is, but what do you think is hinky?"

"It's about Molly."

"Your so-called best friend," Roxie put in dryly.

"Why do you and Adrienne keep calling her that?" And, yeah, she'd used the phrase while talking to herself, but she figured her sisters were the ones that put those words into her head when it came to Molly.

"Because she's not good for you," Roxie said with a shrug. "I know, I know, we don't have to like every single one of your friends, but it doesn't make it any easier to see the two of you together. Not that we ever see you together since she doesn't like to slum with the Montgomerys."

"That's not nice. She's not slumming with us. We're not lower class. We're mostly blue collar, sure, but she's not like that." Even as she said the words, Thea wasn't sure she was being entirely truthful with herself.

"Whatever. I know we're not lower class or whatever the fuck Molly thinks we are. It's not that. It's how she treats you."

"What are you talking about?" Thea picked at wet flour on her hand, frowning.

"She's constantly putting you down, Thea."

"She does not." She paused. "Well, I don't think she means anything by it."

"Listen to yourself, Thea. Don't make excuses for her. Every time you're near her, you shrink in on yourself as if you don't want to become too big of a target. She's totally passive-aggressive. And she's damn good at it. It wasn't until recently that I felt like the gloves had come off and I could actually step back and see it clearly. She comments on your *little bakery*, about the flour on you, the fact you have curves and have to work for a living."

"It's not what you think. Not really. She doesn't do that."

But Molly's words came back to Thea, confusing her as she remembered the things her friend had said to her over the years.

"It's not…it's not that bad."

"Thea…"

"No, because if it's that bad, then what kind of person am I that I could be her friend for all these years? She says stupid stuff that hurts me, but she doesn't do it on purpose.

She *can't* be doing it on purpose, or she's far crueler than I thought possible. I don't think I'd be happy with who I am if I've really let her put me down like that for years. So that can't be what she does." It was circular reasoning at its finest, but she knew that Molly hadn't always been this way, hadn't always been the person who could make Thea question everything.

"Maybe she's not cruel. Maybe that's just who she is, someone who feels better about herself by putting others down. But that's a different kind of meanness and cruelty, right?"

Thea let out a breath. "I don't know. I just don't know. She showed up at my date with Dimitri this weekend." Thea hadn't meant to blurt out that last part, but maybe she needed to.

"Are you fucking kidding me?" Roxie's eyes widened. "Like, actually showed up at that fancy place you were so excited about?"

"Yes. It's apparently *one of her places*. Not that I knew that. Not that Dimitri knew that, since neither of us can actually afford it."

"What did she do?"

Thea winced. "Well, she came over to the table, made a few comments about how surprised she was to see us. Considering it's not our usual place, I got that. Then because she said something about dining alone…"

Roxie groaned. "Tell me you did not invite Dimitri's ex-wife to join you for dinner. Because I get that you and

Molly know each other, but there will always be that sense of you being the other woman with her around."

"I know, I know. Too many tangled webs and hurt feelings. Hence why I have a headache. And, no, we didn't invite her for dinner, but I did invite her to stay for a drink because I was stupid and felt bad and didn't want to see her walk away all alone without friends. Dimitri did his best to be cordial with her but didn't engage her in conversation or invite her to sit down. That was all me, and because I can't put the idea that she's his ex and my friend in the same category, I asked her to join us for a drink. She did, but just that. She didn't eat with us, and we didn't see her again. But then she made a comment about Dimitri's allergy, and I got confused all over again." Thea met Roxie's gaze. "I think she lied to me, Rox. That night and before about the shellfish. And I don't know why or what to do about it."

Roxie held up her hand. "Wait. What about the shellfish? You mean the fact that Dimitri had that reaction when you cooked for him? How is that connected to her?"

Thea explained about the day that Molly had come into the bakery and mentioned what she thought was Dimitri's favorite dish.

"That bitch! She tried to kill her ex-husband. That's what you're saying. She tried to *kill* him and make you the culprit."

Thea's eyes widened. "No. No way. It wasn't that bad. We caught it in time, and he normally wouldn't have even had a bite of the food since he always checks things first, but I was being silly and trying to be romantic about it. I don't think Molly tried to kill him. But I think…I think she wanted to somehow prove she knows him better and put me down in the process. And because of that, I don't know what to think."

Thea looked down at her hands, at the dough under her fingernails and the burn marks along her fingertips. She did her best to keep from comparing herself to others since she couldn't put her next foot forward if she were constantly looking to the side, but she couldn't help but think about the little comments Molly had made about her hands. How her friend—or the woman she'd *thought* was a friend— would mention how she was off for a manicure, something Thea needed but never got because of money and time.

"It's always the little things…" Thea whispered.

"Conveniently forgetting and remembering a deadly allergy isn't a little thing."

Thea pressed her lips together, her head pounding. "You're right. But I don't like what it all means. Or at least what it *could* mean."

Roxie looked at her for a moment, raising a single brow. "You know, something sounds fishy, and I'm not just talking about the shellfish."

Thea groaned. "Really? That's the joke you're going for when I'm having a crisis of friendship or faith or love or all three at once?"

"I can't help it. Your so-called friend sounds a little… shellfish to me."

Roxie grinned, and Thea put her head in her hands, realizing too late that she was smearing dough all over her skin.

"Crap." She went to wash her hands and face, then went back to finishing up her dough so it could rest overnight and not ruin the whole batch.

Thea looked over her shoulder as Roxie laughed. "You need to stop with the fish jokes. This is serious."

"I know. Sorry. I guess I'm just coming out of my shell." They both laughed, tears threatening to stream down Thea's face as she finished up the dough and set it in the fridge to rest overnight. Brioche was tricky, but she knew what she was doing, even with some unexpected resting in the middle of her prep.

"You're a dork, but I love you." Thea rewashed her hands and cleaned up after herself, gesturing for Roxie to meet her up at the corner table in the front area of the bakery where they could talk. She'd been keeping up with the goings-on up front while she stressed out and worked her hands sore doing prep. Her two staff members were working hard, as well, but the place hadn't been busy for the past hour or so, which was okay since it was the normal lull. Moments where they could catch up for the next rush were needed—expansion or not.

Thea checked in with her staff then went back to the table where she and Roxie wouldn't be overheard, bringing two cups of tea with her.

"Thanks," Roxie said, taking the mug from Thea and blowing across the top. "I love Abby's teas. I mean, I love your coffees and cakes, too. But tea sounds perfect right now."

"I know. I'll always be grateful that she moved into the

building because our partnership works perfectly." She let out a sigh and sipped a bit since it was still too hot to gulp like she wanted to. "I'm so confused, Roxie."

"I bet. There's something off with that woman, Thea. I know you don't want to hear it, but from the outside looking in, it's like she's trying too hard to make you and Dimitri happen so she can watch you fall apart. Or maybe she's not that smart and is *trying* to be okay with you and Dimitri being a thing, but also realizes that she's not the center of attention anymore. I don't know."

"I don't know either. That's the problem. There are a hundred different possibilities for why she's doing what she's doing. When I really look at everything that's happened. But those answers running around in my head all say that something is off, and I have a lot of thinking to do."

Roxie reached out and gripped Thea's hand. "What about Dimitri? I know he's not far from your thoughts when it comes to what Molly's trying to do. What are *your* plans when it comes to him? Are you going to tell him what you think could be happening with her?"

"I think I need to." She sipped again. This time, the tea had cooled enough that she could taste more of the peppermint she loved. "Damn it," she whispered into her mug. "How did this get so complicated? It doesn't make any sense."

"It does if you're a spoiled brat who pushes at people when you don't get what you want."

Thea winced. "Every word you just said is true in retrospect, but she's always been so nice to me. We've been friends for years, have supported one another, have held one another when things got hard. We might not have similar friends other than Dimitri, but I thought we had more than what she's reducing this to." If that's what Molly was doing. Maybe Thea was overthinking everything because she hadn't been able to sleep. Maybe things weren't as bad as she thought.

"People grow out of each other. Sometimes, you can't help it."

The way her sister said those words, she had a feeling Roxie was talking about more than Molly, but Thea didn't pry. Not when she was trying to deal with her own messes.

"I just need to think some more about what's really going on with Molly and what's true versus what my brain thinks is happening because I'm confused. As for Dimitri?"

She let out a breath, unable to voice the words.

"As for Dimitri?"

"I love him." She whispered the words, a little startled she'd said them at all.

"I know you do." Roxie's words jolted her.

"How could you know when I haven't been able to think the words?"

"Because I see the way you look at him. And the fact that this whole thing with Molly is making you think about you and Dimitri—together and separately... You're not sad that you might not have Molly in your life. You're worried about the choices you made to be her friend and the choices you're going to have to make to keep Dimitri in your life."

Thea's brows lifted. "That's very insightful for someone who used to get Backstreet Boys and NSync mixed up."

Roxie narrowed her eyes. "It was only the backup ones. I knew Brian and Lance. They were the only two that mattered."

"Sure, honey." That made both of them laugh, and Thea unwound just a little and finished her tea with her sister, relaxing just a bit more when she hadn't thought she would be able to.

Roxie hugged her hard before she left, kissing her on the cheek. "Talk to him, Thea. He's yours. You know? Don't run away because you're scared of what could happen with Molly. She's...well, something is wrong with her. You know?"

"I do." And that was the problem, wasn't it?

"Thea? There's a delivery here, but I think it's wrong."

Thea looked over at Lucy, her staff member, and frowned, glancing at her phone. It seemed they were early, or she would have been back there to take care of it. "I'll go check it, but why do you think it's wrong?"

"It looks like a different brand or something. I don't know, but I figured you should be the one to take care of it."

"Thanks, Lucy. I'll head back."

"No problem, Thea. Hey, Roxie."

"Hey, Lucy," her sister said with a smile. The Montgomerys were a fixture at their businesses, and everyone knew each other decently.

"I'm going to go deal with this guy," Thea said, frowning.

"I'll go with you," Roxie said. "You know how they try to

intimidate the little lady sometimes. Having two of us might help."

As Thea understood, she nodded before heading to the back where the delivery man was trying to unload cases of flour. The wrong flour. The far more expensive flour that was out of her budget and not needed for her particular recipes.

"Hi, I'm Thea Montgomery, and I own Colorado Icing. Where's Wyatt, my usual delivery man?"

"Out sick. I'm here with your order. Your girl who came out here earlier wouldn't sign for it, and I don't have all day. I'm running behind thanks to Wyatt's lazy ass."

What a charmer.

"Let me see the invoices because, unfortunately, your day just got longer. This isn't the flour we ordered. The flour we always order."

"Don't know what you usually order. Don't care. I have what I have, and you're the one that ordered it."

Thea let out a breath, trying not to get too angry. Roxie tapped her foot next to her but remained silent. They were better when they worked as a team and only one of them spoke. That way, the man figured Thea wasn't weak or some other patronizing crap that she'd have to deal with.

"Let me see the papers."

"Fine. Here." He tossed the dirty clipboard at her, and she frowned at the names listed. Yes, it was her bakery, yes, that was her name, but there was an astronomical delivery change fee as well as the flour she hadn't ordered.

"This isn't right. This isn't what I ordered. I don't know how this happened, but this isn't what I need or want."

"No, lady, you called and changed it. We had your info, and you authorized the higher price and the late-change charge. No idea what you're talking about it not being yours. Take it up with your boss."

"I *am* the boss."

"Then take it up with yourself. Sign the paperwork so I can unload."

Thea shook her head. "I can't use this. I need my normal stuff. Take it back."

"You'll be charged."

"Then I'll take it up with *your* boss." She was seething at this point, now confused for a whole new reason.

"Whatever. Don't give a shit."

"And we'll be sure to mention your rudeness," Roxie said from her side, holding up her phone. "I'm recording, so be nice."

He growled at Roxie before taking his clipboard back with deliberate movements and stomping back to his truck, the flour Thea didn't need going with him.

She shook her head as he drove off, and Roxie stopped recording. "Thanks for the backup. He was an asshole."

"Yup. And there's something hinky about all of this. You know?"

Thea nodded. "Hinky is a good word for it."

A word she'd used when it came to Molly, and now it seemed someone was out to hurt her shop. She thought about her paperwork for the expansion and Molly's reference and couldn't help but wonder if she'd made a mistake.

She had no idea what she was going to do next when it came to anything right then. All she could do was wonder if it was all connected or if maybe she was losing her mind along with everything else.

It didn't make sense. Nothing did right then. And all she wanted to do was text Dimitri and tell him that she missed him.

But first, she had to deal with the flour.

CHAPTER 22

Dimitri grinned as his sister rolled her eyes behind his brothers' shoulders. They weren't kids anymore, but damn if they didn't act like it sometimes. Amelia was a decade younger than Dimitri, but still well past being an adult, and yet she hid behind Devin. Devin was two years younger than Dimitri and tried to shift out of the way so Amelia wouldn't use him as a shield anymore, but their sister was fast and wouldn't let Dimitri get to her. Caleb, younger than Devin but older than Amelia, stayed in place, his arms folded over his chest as the other two moved around, though their sister used him as a shield, as well.

It wasn't as if he were going to throw something at Amelia. He just planned to throw her onto the couch or something since she'd been annoying him. She'd always been one of the boys with them and rough-housed as well as the rest of them. She'd taken his phone earlier to try and text Thea, and since he and Thea were going through a rough patch—something the others didn't know about—he didn't want Amelia to text something that might upset Thea.

Not that his sister would do that on purpose, but even texting kissing and heart emojis right then wasn't a good idea. He and Thea had texted some over the weekend, and he planned to call her that night after he got home. He'd stayed up at Devin's place for the long weekend since everyone had off except Thea that Monday, but he wanted to try and see her either later that night or the next day at the bakery. The holidays were fast approaching, and he wanted to make sure they spent them together rather than them sitting on the odd precipice they were currently on.

"I wasn't going to hit send," Amelia said. "And you're too old to pick me up without hurting your back anyway." She went to her toes and hopped a bit to whisper over Devin's shoulder. "You're almost *forty*."

Devin grinned, his eyes dancing. "Yeah, old man. Shortcake here might be too much for you."

"I'm not that short," Amelia growled. "You're just obscenely large."

Devin *was* pretty big. While all three of the Carr brothers were over six feet tall, Devin was the widest muscle-wise, though Caleb wasn't that far behind. Dimitri's two younger brothers were big, built, and heavily inked— even more so than Dimitri. And all of the Denver Carrs went to Montgomery Ink, though they did because of reputation, not because Dimitri knew the Colorado Springs cousins. The latter was just a happy coincidence.

"Hey? Why are you coming down on me?" Devin said, sidestepping completely so Amelia had to hide behind only Caleb. "I thought you were fighting with Dimitri. I'm the good brother."

That made both Dimitri and Caleb snort.

"Really? The good brother?" Dimitri grinned as he said it.

"Well, okay, fine. Dimitri is the good brother. I'm in the middle." Devin glanced at Caleb, who shrugged.

"I was never charged. So, technically, I'm not the bad brother either." Since that was fact, Dimitri couldn't argue, though Caleb had gotten in trouble for stupid stunts and underage drinking in the past.

That had all changed though when they lost their parents. Not that Dimitri wanted to think about that. It had been a long time ago, and he'd gone through other things in his life that had made him who he was now. Like getting married too young to the wrong woman.

The completely wrong woman now that he was getting to know a side of Molly that he was actually starting to fear.

Amelia let out a dramatic sigh before putting both hands up in the air in mock surrender. "Before you boys get your tighty-whities in a twist because you're too busy comparing who's the badest of the bad boys or most beta or whatever, know that I'm the best and favorite Carr sibling. It was written, and therefore it is known." She lifted her chin, her long, dark hair falling behind her shoulders as she tried to act high and mighty.

That sent the three brothers into deep belly laughs, and Amelia rolled her eyes once again before coming toward Dimitri and wrapping her arms around his waist.

"Sorry for taking your phone. If I had known something was going on between you and Thea to the point it's making you nervous, I wouldn't have teased you like that. I was just going to be a dork with her since I like her so much, but I didn't mean to almost make things worse."

And that was his family in a nutshell. Each of them had been through their own ups and downs, some far more than others, but they were all there for each other no matter what. Yeah, they play-fought and sometimes really went at it, but they had each other's backs.

That's why he was here with them even though he hadn't been able to bring Captain thanks to Molly's schedule. He'd needed his family, and with how careful everyone was being with their own personal lives and what they said about them, he had a feeling they needed him, too. Not that they'd told him what was going on. They would when the time came, but right then, they just needed each other.

And now he needed a beer because that was way too much emotion in his thoughts.

"You didn't do anything wrong. Not really. Thea and I..."

Caleb wordlessly held out an open beer, and Dimitri took it, nodding in thanks. He took a swig, then sighed before he started speaking.

"I love her. I didn't mean to, and it sure as hell would

have been easier to stay away when it came to her and all the other crap in our lives, but I fell in love with her, and I'm afraid she's going to push me away because it's not easy."

"She wouldn't give up like that," Amelia said softly. "Not that I know her all that well, but from what you've said about her over the past few years, she works hard and puts her all into everything she does."

"Business-wise maybe," Devin added, then shrugged when Dimitri glared. "Not saying she'll walk away. I don't know her, Dimitri, but she does put everything she has into her business, and since we're all wired that way, I can't judge her for that. But if your ex is muddling everything up, then maybe walking away is what Thea needs to do to keep sane. From what you said, Molly is acting fucking crazy, bro, and you know I don't use that word lightly. If Thea needs to protect herself and her own sanity because of Molly, then you might have to let her."

Dimitri set down his beer and sank onto the couch, covering his face with his hands. "Jesus. I don't know when and how this got so complicated."

"I'd say around the time you married the giggly socialite who hated your family." Caleb gave Dimitri a pointed look but continued. "What?"

"No, you're right. Molly clearly isn't the woman I thought she was. And that's *after* I thought we'd both changed before the divorce." The others were seated around him now. They had already gone over Molly's weird actions over the past few months, including the shellfish and restaurant incidents. Each sibling had taken their turn with incredulous looks and outright pissed-off attitudes, and Dimitri didn't blame them.

"People change," Amelia said softly. "Just because she's this way now, doesn't mean she was when you married her. I know you're blaming yourself for choosing her, because… hello, in some cases, it totally does reflect on the other person for their choice, but that's not the case this time. You chose someone you thought you loved. You were wrong. And I'm guessing Thea is feeling the same way."

"Add all of that to falling for her best friend's ex, and she probably needs this break." Devin just shrugged when they all looked at him for being so insightful. "What? I know things. And I'm not saying she needs a break from you forever, but you clearly needed Carr family time this weekend, and you got it. Hell, I'm pretty sure you made yourself at home in my guest room."

"It's larger than my bedroom at home. I can't help it."

"We'll find you a new place," Amelia said as she leaned into him. "And not up in Denver like I've been trying to get you to do for so long. Because you clearly need to be down in Colorado Springs near Thea."

"When you see Thea again, can we come, too?" Caleb asked, and Dimitri blinked.

"Huh?"

"She owns a bakery. I feel like we should get to know her bakery just like we should get to know her."

Amelia snorted as Devin punched him, and Dimitri just grinned.

"How do you stay so in shape with your sweet tooth?" Dimitri asked.

"First, we all have sweet tooths. Teeth? Whatever. We're Carrs. It's in our sweet blood." Caleb grinned. "Not to be mistaken for sweet breads, which is gross. And, secondly, I work out. A lot. Because I like cake. Cake is my friend."

Dimitri just shook his head as his siblings discussed their favorite cookies and cakes, listening to them while trying to think of what he was going to say to Thea when he saw her next. He'd needed this time with his family so he could remember who he was and where he'd come from. It reminded him why he taught at the school he did, why he dealt with dress codes, and why he stayed down in the Springs. Because that was the life he'd made, and he wanted Thea to be a part of that life.

Meaning, he needed to speak to her.

And talk to Molly to make sure she knew the boundaries he had to put in place. The ones he should have established to begin with.

"You should go," Devin whispered while Caleb and Amelia were fighting about something unimportant. That's how they all dealt with each other: dramatics, loud voices, hard hugs, and support. One more reason Dimitri had come to his brother's place for the weekend.

"You kicking me out?" Dimitri asked dryly.

"No. Never. You're always welcome here, and I know I'll see you again in a couple days for the holidays, but you need to go see Thea. Text her, call her, whatever. But see her.

Soon. Before it's too late because you didn't say the things you should have."

Dimitri frowned, staring at his brother. "Why are you talking to me like you have experience with this?"

Devin's gaze went emotionless, and he shrugged as if he hadn't a care in the world. "I read. And those Marvel movies have a lot of emotion. I mean, the fight between Captain and Tony broke me."

Dimitri knew his brother was lying, but he let the other man keep doing so. When the time was right, Devin would spill. They always did.

"Team Captain forever," Dimitri said, getting up off the couch.

"Team Captain!" the other three said at once then started laughing. They were all a little off their rockers, but they were his family. He wouldn't have them any other way.

"I'm going to head home and call Thea on the way. It's an hour drive, so that should give me time to think about what I need to say before I actually make the call."

Amelia bounced toward him, giving him a hard hug. "Go get your girl. I can't wait to hang out with her." She kissed his cheek, and he did the same to the top of her head. She was his baby sister even if she wasn't such a baby anymore.

"Don't fuck up," Caleb said before pounding him on the back and hugging him even harder. He was pretty sure between Caleb and Devin, Dimitri was going to end up with a broken rib or four.

Devin walked him out, helping him with his bag, though Dimitri could have done it on his own.

"Don't fuck up."

Dimitri just shook his head. "Caleb already said that."

"Bears repeating. Bring her to dinner when you can. I know she works long hours, and with this potential expansion you were talking about, it'll get harder timing-wise, but we want to get to know her. She makes you happy, bro. Don't lose that."

Dimitri nodded, his throat a bit tight, and got into his car, waving at his family as he pulled out of the driveway. Thankfully, the roads were clear, and there wasn't another storm predicted for over a week. They weren't going to have a white holiday, but they'd have less ice and snow on the roads, something he didn't mind in the least.

He got on I-25 and headed south toward the Springs, tapping his fingers on the steering wheel as he tried to figure out what he was going to say to Thea other than that he loved her. He could do that, *should* do that, but it wasn't time yet. Not when things were so uncertain.

"Maybe telling her would make things certain for her," he muttered to himself.

He'd tell her, maybe not tonight if he got to see her, but soon. Because he didn't want to lose her. But then again, he didn't want to overwhelm her either. It was a lot to deal with, and he already came with so much baggage it wasn't even funny. He was damn lucky she'd even given him a chance.

He let out a breath and used the keypad on the steering wheel to call Thea. When she answered on the second ring, he blew out such a relieved breath, he figured she heard it.

"Dimitri."

"I'm heading home from Devin's now and...can I come over? I miss you so damn much, Thea. I know we need to talk, and we will, but I just need to see you." He hadn't known what he was going to say when he called her, but as soon as the words left his lips, he knew they were the right ones.

"I was waiting to call so I didn't interrupt your time with the family. I need to see you, too, Dimitri. Can you come over? Do you have Captain?"

"Molly had him out for grooming when I went to pick him up, so I missed my weekend." He was still bitter about that and had a feeling she'd done it on purpose.

"That bitch. And, Jesus, she just had him at the groomer's. It's like she's finding excuses to get him out of the house. Bitch."

His eyes widened. "Thea?" He'd never heard her talk about Molly that way, even when Molly had started to be more passive-aggressive than usual. The fact that he'd just thought that last sentence spoke volumes about how well Molly had been hiding her true self.

"Come over. I need to hold you and tell you all the crap that's been going on. Because, Dimitri? It's a whole load of crap."

"I'm forty minutes away," he said.

"Don't speed. Stay safe and come home to me."

He let out a shaky breath. "I miss you, babe."

"Miss you, too. And I miss Captain. Can I go over to

Molly's and steal him? Dognapping isn't too bad of a crime, is it?"

He squeezed the steering wheel, trying to stay in control so he didn't get in an accident since people were speeding by him on this one curve that most people drove too fast on.

"I'll get him tomorrow night since it's too late tonight." It was just after dinner time, but he knew he and Thea needed to talk before he went and saw his ex.

"Have him stay here with me. I...I don't want him with her."

"I'm almost there, baby. You need to tell me what happened to make you react like this, though."

"Not when you're driving."

"Worrying about what it could be is just going to make it harder."

"I think Molly is actually trying to push us apart. She's pushing us together so she can look like the bigger person while tearing at us so we break apart, and she ends up on top. It's insane, but after she lied about the shrimp and then all those little remarks over time...it's just weird."

He sighed, looking at the mile marker and wishing he were already there rather than so far away. "I think you and I are on the same page. Jesus, Thea. What a mess."

"It gets worse." She told him about the flour delivery and how a woman had called to change it. "I don't know if it was her, and it's probably a stretch, but seriously, it sounds like someone is out to get me. And that sounds delusional. But she's the only one I know who might do something like that to get back at me for some slight. And doing her ex-husband isn't just any slight."

Dimitri wanted to groan and close his eyes at that, but since he was driving, he resisted. "First, it's not delusional or paranoid if they really are out to get you." She laughed, but he knew it wasn't a full one. "Second, she has no right to feel that way. Not with the words and actions she's used in the past to put us together. Yes, now we know it might have all been a lie, but that's on her. Third, you're not just doing me, and we both know that. Though the doing is nice."

"The doing is more than nice." She paused for a moment. "Come home, Dimitri."

He didn't comment on the fact that she'd called her home, *his* home. That was one more step for them, even in just word choice. "I'll be there soon. Why don't you tell me what kind of cupcakes you're making tomorrow, so we can think of good things. And when I get to your place, we can talk about what we're going to do next."

"I was thinking lemon, even though it's such a summer flavor. I just need a little sunshine."

"You can make two kinds. Summer and winter and make it a thing."

"Cider cupcakes with lemon ones, as well? Think of the decorating I could do with the frosting."

"Now I'm hungry. Maybe I made the wrong choice."

"There's never a wrong choice when it comes to cupcakes."

He smiled. "You need that on a shirt."

"Or a mug. Totally writing it down. How much longer?"

"Twenty minutes."

"Let's talk about brownies then."

By the time he pulled into Thea's driveway, he was hungry *and* horny. Oddly, not the first time when it came to Thea Montgomery. He turned off the car and got out, only to find her jumping toward him. He caught her in his arms and held her close, needing her taste, her touch, *her.*

"I missed you," he whispered against her lips.

"I missed you so much." He kissed her again. "Make love to me, Dimitri. We'll make our plans, figure out what's wrong and why everyone keeps doing the things they're doing, but make love to me first."

He nipped at her lip. "Here? Outside?"

She wrapped her legs around his waist and grinned. "It's a little chilly. What would Little Dmitri say?"

He rocked himself gently against her, aware it wasn't quite late enough for people to be asleep and anyone could look out of their window at any moment.

"Let's go inside and play adult Twister, just without the mat."

"Deal."

He locked his door and carried her inside, locking the house door behind them, as well. He carried her to the bedroom, just holding her as she rested her head on his shoulder. They were both tired, but from the way neither of them wanted to let go of the other, he knew they needed tonight more than ever.

"I want you," he whispered against her neck.

"Then have me. I'm all yours."

Dimitri could barely hold back, then again, when it came to Thea, he usually had that problem. He kissed her softly when they reached the edge of the bed, needing her taste. He'd missed her so damn much, and he couldn't find the words to make sure she understood that. And because he couldn't, he'd find a way to tell her with his hands, his body, just him.

They stripped each other slowly, as if they were relearning one another. He loved the soft curves of her body, the heavy weight of her breasts, the way her hips flared out, and the fact that her thighs were thick and perfect when they wrapped around his waist...and his face.

"I know we usually take our time with foreplay and we're forever teasing each other," Thea began, wrapping her hand around the base of his cock. He swallowed hard, trying to focus on her voice and not her touch. "But can you just get inside me? Next time, we can go slow and do all the things we love to do, but I need you in me. I missed you, Dimitri. I just...I need you."

He leaned forward even as she held him, pressing a gentle kiss to her lips. "You read my mind. Lay on your stomach on the bed. We can still play...just how we like."

Her pupils dilated, and she squeezed him one last time—making him wince—then went to the bed. She gave him a coy look over her shoulder before crawling to the middle and laying down. Her gaze tracked him as he went to the dresser and got out a condom, sliding it over his dick. He ignored the other toys they each had in there—him having left a few new ones for the two of them—and shut the drawer. Then he walked back to the edge of the bed and crawled over her, though he knelt to the side of her legs.

He slid his hand between her legs, and she shivered.

"Already wet."

"Always with you." As he was always hard, he liked that. No, he *loved* that. Loved her. And he would tell her. After.

He tapped her thigh. "Legs together."

She looked at him strangely. "What?"

"Put your legs together. It'll make it feel even tighter." He winked, and she licked her lips before doing as he asked.

Then he settled over her and slowly slid into her. She lifted her ass ever so slightly to give him better access, and he almost lost himself at the first stroke.

"You're so damn tight like this."

She panted into the bed, "I...I don't think I've ever done it this way. I...you feel so big."

He held onto her hips, his thumbs playing with her crease as he shifted his hold. "I'll go gentle."

"Don't. I don't want gentle. Not tonight. Not this time."

So he didn't give her gentle. He slammed into her before pulling out and doing it again. She met him thrust for thrust, squeezing her thighs together as he fucked her...as they made love.

And when he was close, he knelt over her, using his core muscles to pull her up with him. It forced her to spread her legs slightly, and soon, her back was to his front, his hand over her pussy, and his other over her breasts.

She turned her head, capturing his mouth, and he slid in and out of her. The angle was just perfect enough that he could do this, though if she were any shorter, it wouldn't have worked. He'd never felt this close to her, never felt as if they were connected far beyond their bodies.

But they were.

And from the look he caught in her eyes, she knew it, too.

Her arms reached behind them, pulling him even closer, spreading his cheeks at the same time. And because he was so deep inside her, she was able to probe the crease of his ass, but not any farther.

"Next time," he growled into her neck. "Next time, you can play."

Then she fell to her hands, looking over her shoulder with such a fierce look, he knew she was close to the edge. With one more push, they'd both fall into the abyss. "Deal."

He thrust into her hard once more, and she came around him, sending him over the edge, as well. He shouted her name, gripping her hips so hard, he was afraid he'd leave bruises, so he let go but hovered over her back, needing her touch, her heat, her everything.

He needed her.

And now that he had her, he was never letting go.

And if he were lucky, she'd never want him to.

CHAPTER 23

The next day, Thea was sore in all the right places and wanted to go back to her house and get back into bed next to Dimitri. She'd left him there since she had to wake up so early, and he had planned to head back to his place to shower and grab some things before coming to the bakery.

Later, they would go and pick up Captain and possibly confront Molly. The idea that it might feel as if they were ganging up on the other woman had occurred to both of them, but they needed to be a united front against what had been happening under their noses.

Molly was not a nice person.

And that meant she wasn't going to be in their lives.

Even if it hurt.

And, hell, it already hurt, and it was going to hurt more. But there was something unhealthy about the way Molly was in their lives at the moment, and they had to fix that. Yes, they. Not just Dimitri, who wanted to break ties completely. He'd already tried with the divorce, but between Captain and Thea, he hadn't been able to.

Now, it was Thea's turn.

Because Thea could finally see beneath the veneer of the woman to who Molly might have always been. And if she and Dimitri thought things were complicated now, well....it was just going to get worse once they spoke to his ex.

Maybe it was all a misunderstanding. Maybe everything that had happened recently wasn't connected at all, and it was all just a huge error.

Or maybe it was something far worse.

"Thea?" Carter reached out over the counter and gripped her hand, startling her. "What's wrong? You've been standing there watching your coffee cup for a few minutes without saying anything."

She blinked up at her brother-in-law and tried to smile. "I didn't realize I was lost in thought that much. Usually, I can multitask when I think."

Carter studied her face, his eyes searching. He was such a quiet man, though he could make her laugh. She didn't know him well because he was hard to get to know, not because she didn't want to. She knew he loved her sister, saw it in the way he moved around Roxie as if she were his everything, but Thea didn't know if that was enough.

Considering that she hoped Dimitri looked at her the way Carter did with Roxie—albeit with a little less sadness she didn't understand—she hoped that love was enough.

After a moment, Carter sat back and gave her a nod. "Well, usually if you're thinking, you're dealing with dough and kneading or mixing ingredients you know like the back of your hand. Dealing with hot liquid might take a little more attention, hence the standing still with coffee. Either that, or what you have on your mind needs more of you than just the part."

"You sound like you know a lot about thinking on the job."

Carter shrugged before taking a bite of his croissant. He chewed, swallowed, and wiped his mouth before answering. "Lots of time to think when you're under a car. Most of my attention is on my hands, but there's always a part of me that can think about what needs to be done or what hasn't been done yet."

For some reason, she didn't think Carter was talking about a to-do list at the shop, but she didn't pry. The fact that he was talking so freely to her just then surprised her.

"Do you want to talk about it?" he asked after a moment. "I'm not the best with answers, but I'm a decent listener. Sometimes, you just need to talk, you know?"

She almost asked him what was on *his* mind but stopped. What was going on between him and Roxie was between them. And Thea wanted her sister to talk to her, not Carter. Not because she didn't care about her brother-in-law, but because she didn't want to betray her sister by getting any news from another source. Loyalty and love went hand in hand, but it made things tricky when there could be secrets that needed to be kept...or spilled.

"I'm okay." He gave her a look. "I *will* be okay."

"So, I don't have to punch Dimitri for you? Because I know Shep and Mace could easily do it, but Shep got to be all big-brotherly toward Mace, and I haven't had my chance yet."

Thea couldn't help but smile. "You want to act like my big brother?"

He shrugged again. "Of course. I might not be a Montgomery, but I married one. We stick together, right?"

She blinked back unexpected tears. "Yeah, we do. And, Carter? You're totally a Montgomery. Don't let anyone tell you differently."

"I can do that."

She smiled again. "Okay, I'll let you eat. I need to go in the back and deal with my damn oven. It's been acting up today, and I don't have time for that. Not today." She had the afternoon off to be with Dimitri and didn't want to waste time, but if she couldn't get a repairman in soon after she checked it out, she was screwed.

Carter wiped his mouth again and put his napkin on his plate. "I'm all done. Why don't I take a look for you."

"You fix cars. Not ovens."

"True, and I'm not pulling the little lady routine either. I'm just good at fixing things. Most things, anyway." He shook his head and, once again, she had to wonder if he meant something far deeper than what they were actually talking about. "Anyway, I've had to tinker with our oven at home a few times since we need a new one but it's not in the budget right now. And I had to do it growing up at home when my mom didn't want to part with her favorite appliance."

Thea snorted. "I have a favorite oven, too, though that one's working just fine." She knocked on the wood paneling on their way back to the kitchen. "Knock on wood, right? Have you ever dealt with a professional convection oven?"

"Once. You're the one with the experience when it comes to those, but if I can help, then it'll save you time and money, right?"

"I'll pay you in pastry if you can fix it."

Carter grinned. "You do that, and I'll have to work out more if I want to keep in my jeans." He patted his no-doubt rock-hard abs. Roxie's husband was one attractive man, and Thea figured he could indulge in a few more pastries if he wanted—not that she'd say that aloud.

The two of them made their way back to the kitchen where her oven lay quiet, annoying her. She'd made do with her other ones, but she was seriously pissed off.

Carter frowned, taking a look at it before bending down. "So, it's not heating?"

"It's heating for like five minutes, then it stops. I don't get it."

He went to the side of it and looked around, not touching anything before stiffening and standing quickly. "This looks tampered with."

She froze herself. "What?"

There was a hissing sound, then a loud boom that shook the floor beneath her feet. Carter was suddenly on top of her, slamming her hard into the floor as the wall behind the oven caught fire, flames dancing along the ceiling and over her precious countertops.

But that wasn't why Carter had pushed her way.

No, because there were other flames, closer flames, ones that burned and singed and made her scream. Ones that flowed exactly where she and Carter had been standing.

He'd pushed her out of the way, but her arm hurt, and she'd hit her head. Then smoke filled her lungs, and others screamed around them. She tried to push at Carter but he didn't budge, and she was having trouble focusing. She called his name and knew that others were doing the same around her, but they were both in trouble, both hurt. And Roxie's husband had not only saved her life but had risked his in the process.

When the sprinklers went on, the fire died, but she couldn't think, couldn't breathe, she couldn't do anything.

Instead, the sirens came, along with Shep, Adrienne, Ryan, and Mace from the tattoo shop, as well as Abby from her tea shop. Then she saw Dimitri, horror on his face as he went to his knees beside her. He was calling her name, but she couldn't hear it, and she knew something was wrong. Something was terribly wrong.

She wondered if she'd lost everything. Because no matter how hard she fought, it all seemed to be slipping away, one flame, one choice at a time.

HOURS LATER, Thea found herself lying in a hospital bed, a bandage on her arm, another scratching at her chin. She was damn lucky that nothing else was wrong with her, and she knew it. But she still couldn't stop shaking.

Her bakery. Her future. Her work.

Not gone, but hurt.

Her body hurt.

And Carter...she sucked in a breath. She couldn't think about Carter without wanting to scream or hit something. He'd only been in the kitchen to help her, and if she'd been standing where he had been like she planned, she would have gotten hurt far worse.

"Thea? Talk to me." Dimitri sat next to her bed, holding her unbandaged hand. "Are you feeling dizzy? Do you need me to get the nurse?"

She looked over at him, studying the lines of his face. The new creases that had come when he'd seen her on the floor under Carter, smoke in the air, and water drenching the floor and every part of her shop.

"I'm not hurting. Tell me again what happened? I mean, after the explosion."

Dimitri squeezed her hand gently, then leaned forward to kiss her temple. She closed her eyes, trying to take in his scent buried beneath the smoke in her nostrils and the antiseptic stench of the hospital.

"We came in when we heard the fire alarm." Mace sat on her other side, Adrienne by him, holding his hand tightly. "We told your staff to get any customers out of the building, as well as our space and the others in our lot just in case. No one else got hurt. Just you and Carter."

Thea closed her eyes tightly, willing the tears to go away. "And he'll be okay?" she whispered. "He has to be okay."

Adrienne leaned forward and rested her forehead on Thea's leg, her sister's body shaking just like hers was. Then she sat up, looking directly into Thea's eyes as she answered.

"He's in the ICU with a concussion, a broken right arm from how he fell, apparently, and second and third degree burns on the right side of his body. It's less than thirty percent, but it's still enough that they're going to watch for infection and keep him in the hospital for a while."

"I...I can't believe he got hurt because of me."

Dimitri glared at her before schooling his features. "It wasn't your fault. None of this is your fault."

If only she believed that. She wasn't sure she'd ever forgive herself if Roxie lost Carter because of her oven, because of *her*.

"Mom and Dad are with Roxie, making sure she's not alone. Shep, too. Shea has Livvy and Daisy at their place, keeping up with things there as well as answering any questions from the media that come in. Or, in her case, ignoring it but keeping everything organized for us. Mace and I are heading over there soon to help her. We just wanted to stay with you a bit."

Thea reached out and gripped her sister's hand. "I'm okay. I'll be okay. I know there will be questions and I'll have to talk to the police and my insurance company and everything but...thank you for being here. And for being here for Carter."

Dimitri kissed her temple again. "Landon, Abby, Ryan, and Kaylee are around as well, though they're helping with any on-site issues and bringing food and coffee to those who need it. They're all looking for something to do, I think. We're all looking."

Thea looked at the bandages on her hands and wondered what she was going to do now. She'd almost died, and Carter had come even closer. Yet in the end, that wasn't the whole of it. Once she was back on her feet, she would have to go to Colorado Icing and see what could be salvaged. From there, she'd have to restore and possibly rebuild. Her expansion loan paperwork might be thrown entirely out the window at this point, and the next phase of her dreams and her bakery might be over before they started.

She was just grateful that no one else had gotten hurt, though she'd never forget the feeling of Carter lying on top of her, his body limp after he'd slammed into her as the flames licked at their skin.

The heat of it was a clear memory, so vivid she could almost feel it against her skin where the burns beneath her bandages lay. She had second-degree burns on her arm and a cut on her chin from flying debris.

It could have been so much worse.

"I can't believe I almost lost you," Dimitri whispered.

"I'm still here." She swallowed hard. "But I don't know how."

He blinked. "What do you mean?"

"Carter noticed that something was wrong at the last

moment and pushed us both out of the way. What if he hadn't noticed in time?"

"Don't think about things like that," Mace said quickly. "You can't. If you do, you'll go in circles and end up hurting yourself more."

Mace squeezed Adrienne's knee, and Thea knew he was thinking about the events that had led to her sister's attack just a short time ago. So much pain, so much fear, and yet so little time had passed.

"Carter noticed something, but what?" She looked at the man she loved, biting her lip. "What if it wasn't an accident with the oven, Dimitri? What if...what if it was on purpose?"

Mace and Adrienne cursed under their breaths while Dimitri just stared at her. She knew all four of them were thinking the same thing.

Molly couldn't have done this. It had to be an accident.

And yet stranger things had happened.

Far stranger when it came to the Montgomerys.

CHAPTER 24

After Adrienne and Mace went off to check on Shea and see what they could do about their own building for the next day, Dimitri scooted closer to Thea's bed, grateful the others had allowed them some privacy. He knew it wouldn't last long since her parents and Shep made their rounds constantly, but he didn't blame them.

His heart was still racing, and he felt like everything he'd thought he would finally be able to keep in his life was sliding through his fingers like sand.

The authorities had come and gone during the time he and Thea had sat next to one another, not speaking, just touching each other as if it would be the last time, as if it *could* be the last time. He'd listened and tried to make sense of what they were saying, but for now, everything was inconclusive, and it would be a while before anyone could go back into Colorado Icing. That meant they had to wait for answers.

Answers to the questions about who could have done this, and if it had, indeed, been done on purpose.

Jesus.

"I'm okay," Thea whispered.

Dimitri blinked, then looked up at her, wanting to memorize her face all over again. He was afraid he'd lose her if he were away from her for too long. The agonizing wait in the waiting room while the doctors had been working on her had almost killed him. Same as the wait as he'd driven behind the ambulance. Adrienne had ridden with Thea because they were family. But, honestly, Dimitri wasn't sure if he would have been sane enough to sit next to her and not growl or scream. No one had ridden with Carter as they'd needed the space, but Roxie and the rest of the crew had shown up soon after. Cousins and family from around the state wanted to come down, but so far, they were being held at bay until later. Too many Montgomerys in one place could be a bit much, even for him.

"I almost lost you today." He held Thea's hand, playing with her fingers as he tried to formulate his thoughts.

She turned her hand, palm up, and covered his fingers with her own. "I was so scared. So scared about Carter, everything I've worked for, and not seeing you again." She gave him a shaky smile. "But they're getting me my clothes, and I'm going to be released soon. So, I guess that's something. We can wait to hear about Carter with the others. I don't want Roxie to be alone."

He looked up then, letting out a slow breath. "I love you so damn much, Thea Montgomery. I don't know what I would have done if I'd lost you." He stood up, leaned over her, and cupped her face. "I know it's fast, I know everything in the world seems to be pushing us apart, but I don't care. I love you. I don't know when I fell, but I know it was soon after landing on you during Twister when we thought we could try to just be friends. Honestly, I probably started to fall when I saw you in the grocery store, afraid you were hurt but finding out you were just pissed off and in need of ice cream."

She searched his face, and he leaned down, brushing his lips along hers.

"I love you, Thea. I know you might need more time, and I get that. I'll wait. I'll always wait for you. But I can't go another moment wondering if I could lose you again without you knowing how I feel."

She reached between them, putting her bandaged hand over his lips. "I love you, too."

He swore his chest was too small for his heart just then. He kissed her fingers, and she lowered her hand. "Say it again."

She smiled, tears filling her eyes. "I love you, Dimitri. I should have said it before this, you know, but I thought it was too soon, as well."

"Nothing's too soon. Not for us." He kissed her again, careful of the cut on her chin. She was numb now, but he knew it would hurt her soon. "I'm just sorry I waited until we were in the hospital and you were hurt. I wanted to tell you last night, I thought I could finally say the words, but it didn't feel right. Not with how we just wanted to *be*."

Thea's uninjured hand came up to his face, cupping his cheek. "I get it. And this moment, right here? I'm going to remember this feeling. Yes, I'm going to remember everything else that happened today, but it's not going to be all bad. There will be touches of light and warmth in the darkness, and I think that's what I need."

He kissed her softly, aware he needed to stop before someone walked in and found them in a compromising position.

"I love you. I'm never going to stop loving you. I thought my path was one thing, but it turns out it was just a curve for me to find you."

She kissed the corner of his mouth. "Lots of curves and twists for us. And with everything else up in the air, I have a feeling we're not through with them yet."

As if on cue, his phone rang, and he closed his eyes, letting out a curse. "That's Molly's ring."

Her face paled. "I know. You should answer. It could be about Captain."

He looked down at the readout and shook his head. "We need to confront her together about what she's done, but what if she did more than we think?"

Thea ran her hand over her head and winced since she'd done it with the bandaged one. "Answer anyway. Because there's just no way Molly had anything to do with the explosion. I mean, that would make her insane."

Dimitri gave her a look that spoke volumes, but since he

didn't believe Molly knew how to tamper with an oven or would actually do that, he hoped it was all just an accident, and his mind was playing tricks on him.

He answered the phone on the last ring, wishing he'd just let it go to voicemail. "Molly. I'm a little busy right now. What's wrong?"

He knew something was actually wrong from the first sound of her voice. "Oh my God, Dimitri. It's Captain. I can't find him anywhere. I left the door open when I was coming in, and it's so cold out. Oh my God. What if it snows? I can't find him, Dimitri. Captain's gone! Can you come home? Can you come find our boy? Oh God. Captain!"

Molly started wailing, and Dimitri was instantly up, his hand shaking as he tried to force his breathing to slow down.

Shep walked in at that moment, frowning at them, and Dimitri figured his phone's volume was up high enough that both the other man and Thea had heard Molly's words.

"Shit. Molly. Calm down. I'm on my way." She cried some more, and he hung up. "I'm sorry, Thea. I need to go."

She was already trying to get out of bed, but Shep put his hands on her shoulders, stopping her. "I'm coming, too. They're signing me out, and I don't want you to have to go over there yourself. Plus, I love that dog. Captain's your baby."

He kissed her softly, ignoring Shep's warning look. Yeah, Shep's baby sister had gotten hurt, and he was being over-protective, so Dimitri would let it slide this once. Considering he'd be tearing down the walls if Amelia got hurt, he understood. It was all caveman and would annoy Thea to no end, but he got it. He just wouldn't say anything about it.

"You need to stay here. Let me find Captain, and you can get signed out. If for some horrible reason I can't find him by the time you're cleared, then—and only if you're rested—you can come."

She narrowed her eyes. "You can't actually tell me what to do, Dimitri. It doesn't matter if I love you, you don't get to order me around."

"I know, baby. But I need you safe when I go look for him."

Shep cleared his throat. "Thea, stay with me for a bit. Let's get you signed out and dressed. By the time you're all ready to go, Dimitri will probably have found Captain. You know how dogs are, they come right when you call them if they're in love with you like that dog is with Dimitri."

Dimitri kissed her again. "I'll see you soon. I just need..." He let out a breath. "I need to make sure Captain is okay. And with how things are with Molly, I just don't know anymore."

"Go. I'll be right behind you."

He nodded, kissed her again, then headed out of the room after lifting his chin at Shep. He didn't have time to stop by the other Montgomerys and check in with Roxie and the others, but he knew Thea would update him. He wouldn't be surprised if she were already getting dressed, tapping her foot as she waited to get checked out so she could follow him.

On that thought, he was glad she didn't have her car and Shep would have to drive her out if she wanted to come. She'd almost been fucking blown up for God's sake.

He shook his head as he got into his car and made his way to Molly's house. Everything was happening all at once, and it didn't give him any time to think or process. He tried to keep his speed down, but all he wanted to do was get to the house and find his dog. He should have picked Captain up before this, never should have left him with Molly— apartment guidelines or no. He'd never forgive himself if something happened to his golden because of his poor choices and that fucking woman.

Yeah, that damn woman.

He was already blaming her for a lot of mistakes and her downright cruel actions when it came to Thea, and he was just so pissed off that she'd been so careless.

Who the fuck leaves the door open in the middle of fucking December?

He growled to himself, his thoughts turning over and over again in his head as he made his way to her house. It wasn't that far since he was on her side of town, and as soon as he pulled in behind her car, he jumped out of his vehicle and raced to the door.

The door that was once again open with Molly standing inside, her eyes wide and her hands clasped in front of her chest.

"You came. I knew you'd come when I called. You always come. For me. You always do."

He looked at her and knew something was off. And not

just with her current state of mind about Captain. Damn it, he should have seen the warning signs long before this.

"Where have you looked for him? Have you called the neighbors? When's the last time you saw him?"

Molly blinked at him, and her cheek twitched. "How's Thea? Did she...get hurt?" There was something in her voice that he couldn't quite place.

He froze. "I didn't tell you about the bakery."

She tilted her head, unblinking. Seriously, it was fucking creepy. "I heard it on the news. The Montgomerys are everywhere it seems. Too bad about the explosion."

He let out a breath, trying to remain calm. "Where's Captain, Molly? What have you done with him?"

"Me? I've done nothing to our dog. He's gone. I don't know where."

"*My* dog. He's mine, Molly. He was never yours. And I never should have left him here. That was a mistake I won't be making again." There were a thousand different things he needed to say to his ex, another thousand different puzzle pieces he needed to put together if that tingling sensation in his mind were any indication. However, he didn't have time for any of that, not when Captain could actually be hurt or lost.

He turned his back on Molly as he went inside toward the backyard where he could start his search. Out of the corner of his eye, he saw her eyes narrow, but he ignored it. But as he kept moving, he knew he'd made a mistake.

Shocking pain slammed into his head, and he went down to his knees. He blinked, his gaze going fuzzy, and his

mouth filling with a metallic taste. He couldn't quite understand what had happened. As he fell to his back, twisting at
the last second to break his fall, he looked up to see Molly
holding a large wrench, the same one he'd used to help fix
Molly's sink the other day when he'd come back to the
house after seeing Thea.

"Damn it, Dimitri. Why can't you understand?" She
blinked finally, and he felt himself fading. "You're mine. You
chose me. You're. Mine."

He could only thank God that Thea hadn't come with
him. Because if she had, who knew what Molly might
have done.

They'd been wrong. Molly wasn't merely having issues.

She'd lost it completely.

And he had no idea what he could do about it.

Then there was only darkness...and the sound of a dog
whining from the other room.

CHAPTER 25

"*Y*ou should be in bed."

Shep's sharp comment from the driver's seat didn't worry Thea. After all, he'd said it about fourteen times since she'd gotten dressed at the hospital, quickly signed a few papers once the doctor let her go, and jumped into his car. She'd practically pulled him out of the hospital, leaving the others behind. She was worried about Carter and knew that her family could take care of Roxie until Thea got back, but she needed to make sure Dimitri was okay.

Not that she thought he was hurt or anything, but she was leaning more toward the idea that Molly had cornered him into a conversation or situation he didn't want to be in. She had to hope that they were just overthinking everything that her friend had done in the past. Maybe they were seeing things that weren't there, and everything would be fine.

Only now, Thea couldn't get every snide remark, every put-down out of her head. How had she let that go on for so long?

"What are you thinking about so hard over there?" Shep asked as they made another turn.

"The fact that I was so blind to how Molly treated me. It's a cliché, you know? The ex-wife and the former friend. I just...I just can't believe how things got so out of hand and that I didn't see it."

"I don't think that's the case."

"What do you mean?"

"I remember when you met her. I wasn't living here at the time, but I was here for a full month visiting the folks and doing some work at the local shop. Remember?"

"I do." She nodded, her body aching from the fall but still bouncing on the seat as she waited to get to Molly's and see if Dimitri was there.

"She was nice. I mean, I didn't know her all that well and only met her a couple of times, but she's always been part of a different circle than us. We're heavily blue collar, and that's fine with me. You know? She wasn't blue collar. She married someone who was, though, and I guess that surprised me."

"I introduced them." She sighed. "I try not to think about that because everything changed when I did. I knew them both before they got married, and while I didn't know they'd click like they must have if Dimitri married her, I thought they'd make it work."

"And it didn't. That's not on you. Hell, it's probably not on Dimitri's or Molly's shoulders either. Sometimes, marriages don't work, and even though Molly's always been a bit self-centered in my opinion, I thought the divorce was pretty amicable. No fighting from what you told me, no yelling or even complaining when it came to the divorce proceedings."

"You're right. I don't know everything that happened during that time, but from what Dimitri's told me, they just...didn't work. And the divorce went quick. And though he still had Captain at her place, they didn't do anything together after everything happened. But it wasn't like they hated each other."

She paused.

"I think...I think something's wrong with Molly."

"What do you mean?" Shep asked, taking another turn.

"I don't know. She's made small comments about my job or wardrobe over the years, but I don't think she ever meant it as meanly as I believe she's doing now. It's like when she tried to convince herself that Dimitri and I could be good together and even tried to push us together, something snapped."

Shep cursed under his breath. "That might be the case. But it's not like we can figure it out on our own. There's no proof that she had anything to do with the flour or the explosion. But she *did* lie to you a few times in what seemed to be a way for her to sound better than you or at least more connected to Dimitri. It could be she changed her mind about being okay with your relationship."

Thea picked at her bandages, her pain meds starting to wear off. She'd have to be careful, but she couldn't wait to see if Dimitri called her back or not.

"I know." She let out a breath. "If we discount everything else, the idea she was so happy about our relationship was too good to be true. I so desperately wanted to believe it, though, I ignored my instincts. She had a right to be hurt."

"But she didn't have the right to hurt you. Or Dimitri. Just be careful, okay?" Shep parked behind Dimitri's car, and Thea's heart raced. He was here…but he wasn't answering his phone, and she didn't like that.

"Let me go in by myself," she blurted, undoing her seatbelt.

"Uh, I don't think so."

"You can wait right by the car, but I don't want to go in there and bully her. Just in case I'm wrong about everything and she's lashing out verbally because she's hurt. Bringing you in there could only make things worse."

Shep cursed again. "Fine. I'll be leaning against the car in the cold, ready to run in there if something happens. And, fuck, I'll keep an eye out for Captain because, for all we know, Dimitri and Molly are out without reception trying to find that dog. Storm's coming in, and I don't want him to get hurt either."

She leaned over and kissed her brother's cheek, wincing when she pulled at her stitches. He caught the movement and glared, but she hopped out of the car as quickly as she could. Everything was going to be okay. She was just over-reacting because of the explosion and Carter and now Captain being gone. It was all just too much, and as soon as she saw Dimitri, everything would be okay.

And if she kept telling herself that, she'd totally start believing it.

Thea made her way to the front door and knocked, but the door opened without her even trying, as if it hadn't been latched properly. Her heart lifted to her throat, and she turned to look at Shep. He must have seen something on her face because her brother was at her side in an instant.

"What's wrong?"

"The door's open."

"Shit."

"Maybe they left it open when they went looking for Captain. That's what Molly said happened in the first place. How Captain escaped." Only, it felt wrong. It all felt wrong.

"Should we call the cops?" Shep asked, already pulling out his phone.

"We're overreacting." Thea took a deep breath and opened the door fully. "Molly? Dimitri?"

They hadn't been overreacting.

Molly sat on *top* of the dining room table, a wrench in her fist, and her hands over her ears as she rocked back and forth.

"Mine. He was mine. Mine. He was mine."

"Dimitri..." Thea hadn't realized she'd whispered his name until Molly looked up sharply and narrowed her eyes.

"You. He was supposed to be *mine*. He chose me. Now,

he's dead, and it's all your fault. You should have seen that you two weren't meant for each other. You should have *seen*. If you had, he'd have come back to me, and nothing would have been ruined. He wouldn't be hurt." She scratched at her chest with her free hand, the other still holding the wrench. "*I* wouldn't be hurt."

"Jesus Christ." Shep took a step forward, putting his body between Molly and Thea, but Thea was having none of that, not after everything she'd been through.

"Molly. What's going on?" she asked, moving around her brother, who glared down at her. Tough shit. "Where's Dimitri?"

"Does it matter? It never matters. You're the one who did this. It's always been you. The pretty one. The one who looks beautiful without any work. You can eat all you want and not gain a pound. You have parents and siblings, and friends who would die for you. You had everything except Dimitri. And then he didn't want me anymore, and I didn't think I needed him. Then you walked in and *took* him. You took him from me, and now it's all ruined."

There was so much packed into that statement that Thea couldn't keep up. All those digs and slights had been for a reason, but not the ones Thea had thought they were for.

"Molly. Where's Dimitri?"

"It's all your fault."

Thea barely ducked out of the way of the wrench in time.

Shep was already on the phone with the police when Molly launched herself at Thea, but Thea was done. *So* fucking done with this woman and all the guilt she'd carried for what seemed to be something far deeper than anything she could have dreamed.

Shep cursed into the phone and reached out to pull Thea out of the way, but she already had her free hand pulled back and punched into Molly's nose before he could stop her.

Molly hit the floor, her head slamming back, and an enraged scream echoing in the air. Then Molly rolled and tried to kick out, but Thea was already on the other woman, pinning her down. Her hand hurt—of course she'd have to use her burned one—and she was pretty sure she'd popped a stitch, but she was done.

"Stop it. What is the matter with you? Stop it, Molly."

Tears spilled down her cheeks, and she tried to remember the happiness the other woman had brought into her life, only there wasn't as much there as there should have been. Everything was dark and different, and she had no idea what she was doing anymore.

Shep pushed her to the side and pinned Molly down, though she knew he was being gentle. The other woman thrashed, but her eyes looked unseeing, as if she were screaming at something not there. Thea knew that something had gone terribly wrong with the woman who had once been her friend. She didn't know what had happened, but she knew anything they might have had was lost forever, and she could only hope that Molly would be able to find the peace she so desperately craved.

"Find Dimitri," Shep barked. "I've got her. Cops are on the way."

She stood up quickly on shaky legs, her hands damp and tears still streaming down her face. She staggered around the dining room, searching as if she'd be able to find him from where she was though she knew she wasn't truly seeing anything.

Then she saw his foot.

She let out a scream she knew would haunt her dreams and ran to the kitchen where Dimitri lay face-down on the ground, the back of his head wet. He was so still, she was afraid she was too late.

"Dimitri," she whispered. "Dimitri."

He groaned, and it was possibly the best sound she'd heard in her life.

The love of her life turned onto his back and blinked up at her, squinting. "Thea?"

She brushed her fingers over his lips. "Shh, baby. Don't speak. People are on their way to help you. I love you so much."

"I…Molly?"

"Shep has her. Don't move. Be still, just in case you're hurt worse."

"My head hurts like a bitch, but I'm okay." He reached out and cupped her face. "I love you, Thea."

"I love you, too."

And even as the sound of sirens hit her ears, there was a loud commotion, the sound of wood breaking, and then a large ball of golden fur was on them, licking at her face and then at Dimitri's. She pushed Captain out of the way, his whining making her cry even harder.

"It's okay, baby boy. Don't move your daddy. Let's keep him safe."

Captain stood guard over them both, and Dimitri met her gaze, the love and hurt in his eyes evident.

He was safe.

Captain was safe.

And Molly would get help.

And soon, Thea would sleep because she was afraid if she stayed up much longer, something else would happen, and she wouldn't be strong enough for it.

But for now, she was.

CHAPTER 26

*D*imitri once again found himself at the hospital, only he was the one in the bed this time and Thea was the one by his side. His head hurt, and he needed more stitches than Thea, but he was going to be okay. Concussion protocol wasn't going to be easy, but he'd take care of himself and work his way through it.

He still couldn't quite believe everything that had happened, though. So much anger, so much confusion and distrust.

That hadn't been the woman he married. Nor had it been the woman he no longer loved. Something had happened inside Molly to change that, and he didn't have pity or anger toward her, just sadness that it had happened at all. There was nothing he could do to change it, but he also had to learn to deal with what happened.

Molly had a longer road of recovery in front of her than

either he or Thea. Only Carter might have her beat, but even then, he didn't know when—or if—Molly would find peace. Carter was going to heal, was going to be okay.

None of them knew about Molly.

"Today has been a shit day," Shep said from his side. "And now I'm going home to my wife and baby girl. After the yelling and screaming from the folks and the doctors for taking Thea to you, I think I'm done for the day." The other man stood up and gave him a nod. "Take care of my baby sister, Dimitri. I don't want to see another bruise on her."

Thea let out a growl by his side, but Dimitri kept his eyes on Shep. "I will, though I can't make promises."

"I'd say I hate you both, but today's been too long for me to mean it." Thea stood up and hugged her brother while Dimitri lay there, waiting to see when he'd be discharged. "Love you. Thank you for taking me. I don't know what I would have done if…"

She didn't finish the sentence, and even Dimitri had to cough to clear his throat.

"We found him. Captain is doing great and hanging with Dimitri's brothers and sister at your place. We're all going to be fine. Okay?" Shep hugged her again, then walked out, leaving Thea and Dimitri alone in the hospital room.

Devin, Caleb, and Amelia had already been to the room. They hovered, growled, and wanted vengeance, but had taken one look at Thea and just held her close, making sure she knew she was one of them now. She'd given them her keys and said to make themselves at home so they didn't need to get hotel rooms and so they could take care of

Captain. Somehow, it had all worked out, and Dimitri knew there would be time for more questions and answers later.

"Today has been a long day."

Dimitri looked at her, snorting. "You can say that again. There's a storm raging outside, and I'm kind of glad for it, or all the Montgomerys and Carrs would be in this room or in Carter's trying to will everyone to heal up. You should be at home, too, you know. You need sleep."

She shrugged and got into the bed with him. They were probably going to get into trouble with the nurses, but he didn't care, not when he had her warm weight next to him.

He'd almost lost her twice today, and she'd almost lost him. That was too much for anyone.

"Mom and Dad finally went home. Mace and Adrienne are here again with Roxie. They brought her clean clothes and food, and they're going to stay the night with her. There's a guest room area that family can use for that section of the hospital. Carter's awake, but they're doing their best to keep him sleeping a bit more so he can heal up. He's going to be okay, but he's not going to be how he was before the explosion."

"None of us will be how we were before today," he said softly. "But we'll figure it out." He paused. "So, I was dealing with the doctors when the police came to talk to you. Molly really hired that delivery man to mess with your oven?"

She nodded against him, letting out a breath. "Apparently. I don't know all of it, but the inspectors found evidence and were already looking into the man when the guy spilled everything about his connection to Molly and how he thought he was just making the oven not work, not making it dangerous. I don't know what's going to happen to him or Molly. No one thinks Molly or even the delivery guy were really trying to hurt anyone, but that doesn't change the outcome."

It was all too surreal, and they both knew it. But buildings and kitchens could be rebuilt. He, Carter, Thea, and even Captain would be okay. Molly would get help, and the world would continue to move on as they tried to come to terms with everything that had happened that day.

"I love you." There really wasn't much more he could say just then.

She looked up at him. "I love you, too."

Then she kissed him, and he knew everything would be okay. Eventually.

They just needed time to process, to think, to heal, to feel. But he knew that, no matter what, he'd only be able to do it with the woman he loved by his side, the woman of his heart, the woman who stood by him throughout it all.

The only woman that made him feel.

His woman.

His Thea.

Sometime later...

"You know, I'm liking this new uniform of yours," Thea said as she straddled him after work.

"Yeah?"

"Yeah. I mean, I've always loved your ink and, apparently, forearms are another of my kinks, but the fact that the new administration lets you pull up your sleeves and show off your ink makes me happy." She paused. "And a little horny."

"Thankfully, you're wearing a dress then," Dimitri said softly and worked himself out of his pants. She wiggled a bit and somehow got her panties off. He loved how talented she was.

Captain let out a sigh on the other end of the couch, and both Dimitri and Thea laughed. Their golden retriever heaved himself off the furniture—somewhere he wasn't supposed to be anyway, but it was so hard to tell him no these days—and went back to the office where his other bed was.

"I love that dog. Hence why I've always been Team Captain. He knows what needs doing."

Then she was on him, sliding over his dick, her wet heat enveloping him. They'd only just started forgoing condoms, using other birth control before they started a family, and he'd never known sex like this. He was hers, forever, and so fucking sexy.

He kissed her, loved her, and rocked with her as they made love slowly on their couch—he'd moved in right after everything had gone haywire. And when they both came, he held her close, staying inside her so they could hold one another and let their breathing slow.

"I love doing that," she said softly.

"Sex?" Dimitri asked gruffly. "Yeah, I love that, too."

She rolled her eyes, then kissed his cheek. "No, I love kissing you, being with you, and knowing it's not the last time. It's not the first either. It's just *us*. Part of us, part of who we are." She wiggled on top of him, and his eyes crossed. "And I love that we can have sex on a lazy afternoon with only the normal worries of work, family, and little things like world peace."

He grinned at her, then took her mouth again. "Love you, Thea Montgomery. Just saying."

"And I love you, Dimitri Carr. Now, let's get cleaned up so I can practice my next cupcake for you for the reopening."

She winked at him, but he knew she was still upset that it had been over a month now and the bakery was just now ready to reopen, the expansion put on hold for the time being.

He didn't say anything, just cleaned each other up then slowly walked back to the bedroom, *their* bedroom.

This was their life now, one choice after another, but they'd made the ones they needed for them, for what they wanted, needed, and cherished. Together.

He'd been restless before, trying to find his way without knowing who and what he needed to be. Now, he had his woman, his work, and his dog.

His life wasn't perfect, nothing was, but it was pretty damn perfect for him.

EPILOGUE

Thea looked down at her loan paperwork, cursing but trying not to cry. She'd been denied twice. The fire and Molly's efforts in taking her down had left their wounds. Apparently, before Molly had been arrested, she'd indeed turned in a letter to the loan office. Only it wasn't a recommendation. It was a scathing review from a family with money and connections. With Molly dealing with her own issues from behind bars now, however, that letter should have done nothing. However, that paperwork added on to the fire and everything that had gone on meant that the bank didn't see Thea as a good candidate for expansion at the moment. She'd barely been able to get the insurance money to repair her bakery as it was.

Colorado Icing was going to stay as it was for now, and Thea would just have to deal.

She'd just eat a few cupcakes first.

"I'm sorry, babe," Dimitri said, kissing her neck from behind. "I know you really wanted this."

She shrugged as if indifferent, but she knew he saw through the lie. "It's okay. I'll deal." She shook herself, then pulled away. "It's game night anyway, we might as well get to work and have fun. It's an anniversary of sorts, right?"

Dimitri smiled, and while it reached his eyes, she knew he was still sad for her. The expansion had been her dream, and now it was going to be put on hold. But only for a couple of years. She'd find a way to make it work. She wouldn't give up. Not yet.

"It's the first game night at your house since we started dating. Can we end it the same way with Twister?"

She bit her lip. "Only if we do it naked."

"I'm still here, you know," Shep growled. "I mean, look around you when you have a full house on the way. Seriously."

Shea laughed by Shep's side and patted her husband's chest. "Poor baby is so surprised his baby sister and her live-in boyfriend have s-e-x."

"Shush, you."

"Or, what? You'll take away our s-e-x?" Shea fluttered her eyelashes, and Thea laughed. Soon, the house was filled with Montgomerys *and* Carrs. Abby, Ryan, Landon, and Kaylee were there, too. So many people, and so much love and food in the room, she couldn't feel sad about having to wait a couple of years before she expanded Colorado Icing.

The only thing that put a damper on the night was the fact that Roxie and Carter weren't there. They had things to work out for themselves, and Thea was truly afraid they'd never come to game night again.

She pushed those thoughts from her mind, though, knowing they didn't help anyone. Not right then. So, she held out her cheese plate, grinned at the man she loved, and went back into the living room to officially begin their night of fun.

Dimitri was right behind her, his hand on her hip as she stood in her living room with so many people she loved surrounding her. She'd lost a friend this year, one Thea had thought had her back. But Molly wasn't the woman Thea thought she was. Despite the loss, Thea had gained so much more in the end.

She'd gained her love, her future, and the man who made her smile. She'd spent so long looking for her happiness in her work, that she'd left the thought of forevers behind. Now, she had both, even if it took work and wasn't finished yet. But she didn't want it to be finished. She wanted to work hard for Colorado Icing, and Dimitri.

Nothing good ever came with luck, and now she had the two—three if she included Captain—things she loved.

She let out a breath, trying to focus. "Okay, how do we want to do this? What teams?"

"Montgomerys, Carrs, vs others?" Landon asked. "Though I don't know if that evens out."

Ryan snorted. "Yeah, Montgomerys come out of the woodwork it seems."

"He's not wrong," Adrienne said with a laugh.

"Well, what if there was one more Carr?" Dimitri asked, and Thea turned, confused.

"What do you mean?"

Then she froze, and the room went silent as she looked at Dimitri down on one knee, a ring between his fingers. It was a square-cut diamond surrounded by yellow citrine gems and had more diamonds along the band. It was a perfect mix of old and new and she'd never seen anything like it.

"Thea Montgomery, will you be with me until the end of our days? Be by my side and let me be by yours? I know it's fast, and we can spend years on the next step if you want to, but when I saw this ring, I thought of you and I couldn't wait any longer. You said tonight was an anniversary of sorts, and you were right. Will you marry me?" Captain barked from Mace's side. "Captain is asking, as well."

Tears spilled down her cheeks, and she tried to catch her breath. She knew it was too soon, knew they had so much to learn about each other and so many other things that told her to say no. But she couldn't. Not when she knew deep down in her heart that this was the man for her. The man for her forever.

"Yes! Yes, I'll marry you."

Dimitri kissed her then, sliding the ring onto her finger as their families and friends cheered, clapped, and in some cases, cried.

"Looks like we get another Carr," Devin said.

"She'll always be a Montgomery," Adrienne added.

And while she listened, she kissed the man she loved, the

man who would be her husband, and knew she'd made the right choice. They both had.

They'd taken a chance on fate and love, and now they were taking a chance on more...together.

With cheese plates, cupcakes, and a golden retriever on Team Captain by their sides.

THE END

The Montgomery Ink: Colorado Springs series continues
with Jagged Ink.
Roxie and Carter truly need their story.

A NOTE FROM CARRIE ANN

Thank you so much for reading **RESTLESS INK**. I do hope if you liked this story, that you would please leave a review! Reviews help authors *and* readers.

I'm so honored that your read this book and love the Montgomerys as much as I do. Thea and Dimitri's romance was something far different than I'd ever written, and I'm glad I got to write it. I write so many different types of ex wives, husbands, and significant others. Venturing into one where they weren't evil, but hurt in a way no one understood was something I wanted to write. Thea and Dimitri got their HEA and now it's time to see what's next!

And in case you missed it, you can find their brother Shep's romance in INK INSPIRED. Up next is Jagged Ink and I know this book will be hard but worth it. Roxie and Carter are waiting.

And if you loved Mace's sisters from Fallen Ink, don't worry, they're getting their own series with the Fractured Connections series, starting with BREAKING WITHOUT YOU!

Dimitri's family, the Carr's will be getting their own story soon as well. More to come on that!

And if you're new to my books, you can start anywhere within the world and catch up!

Don't miss out on the Montgomery Ink World!

- Montgomery Ink (The Denver Montgomerys)
- Montgomery Ink: Colorado Springs (The Colorado Springs Montgomery Cousins)
- Gallagher Brothers (Jake's Brothers from Ink Enduring)
- Whiskey and Lies (Tabby's Brothers from Ink Exposed)
- Fractured Connections (Mace's sisters from Fallen Ink)

If you want to make sure you know what's coming next from me, you can sign up for my newsletter at www.CarrieAnnRyan.com; follow me on twitter at @CarrieAnnRyan, or like my Facebook page. I also have a Facebook Fan Club where we have trivia, chats, and other goodies. You guys are the reason I get to do what I do and I thank you.

Make sure you're signed up for my MAILING LIST so you can know when the next releases are available as well as find giveaways and FREE READS.

Happy Reading!

Montgomery Ink: Colorado Springs
    Book 1: Fallen Ink
    Book 2: Restless Ink
    Book 3: Jagged Ink

Montgomery Ink:
    Book 0.5: Ink Inspired
    Book 0.6: Ink Reunited
    Book 1: Delicate Ink
    Book 1.5: Forever Ink
    Book 2: Tempting Boundaries
    Book 3: Harder than Words
    Book 4: Written in Ink
    Book 4.5: Hidden Ink
    Book 5: Ink Enduring
    Book 6: Ink Exposed
    Book 6.5: Adoring Ink
    Book 6.6: Love, Honor, & Ink
    Book 7: Inked Expressions
    Book 7.3: Dropout

Book 7.5: Executive Ink
Book 8: Inked Memories
Book 8.5: Inked Nights
Book 8.7: Second Chance Ink

Want to keep up to date with the next Carrie Ann Ryan Release? Receive Text Alerts easily!
Text CARRIE to 24587

ABOUT CARRIE ANN

Carrie Ann Ryan is the New York Times and USA Today

bestselling author of contemporary and paranormal romance. Her works include the Montgomery Ink, Redwood Pack, Talon Pack, and Gallagher Brothers series, which have sold over 2.0 million books worldwide. She started writing while in graduate school for her advanced degree in chemistry and hasn't stopped since. Carrie Ann has written over fifty novels and novellas with more in the works. When she's not writing about bearded tattooed men or alpha wolves that need to find their mates, she's reading as much as she can and exploring the world of baking and gourmet cooking.

www.CarrieAnnRyan.com

MORE FROM CARRIE ANN

Montgomery Ink:

Book 8: Inked Memories
Book 8.5: Inked Nights
Book 8.7: Second Chance Ink

Montgomery Ink: Colorado Springs
Book 1: Fallen Ink
Book 2: Restless Ink
Book 3: Jagged Ink

Montgomery Ink: Boulder
Book 1: Wrapped in Ink

The Gallagher Brothers Series:
A Montgomery Ink Spin Off Series
Book 1: Love Restored
Book 2: Passion Restored
Book 3: Hope Restored

The Whiskey and Lies Series:
A Montgomery Ink Spin Off Series
Book 1: Whiskey Secrets
Book 2: Whiskey Reveals
Book 3: Whiskey Undone

Fractured Connections
A Montgomery Ink Spin Off Series
Book 1: Breaking Without You
Book 2: Shouldn't Have You
Book 3: Falling With You

The Talon Pack:

Book 1: Tattered Loyalties

Book 2: An Alpha's Choice

Book 3: Mated in Mist

Book 4: Wolf Betrayed

Book 5: Fractured Silence

Book 6: Destiny Disgraced

Book 7: Eternal Mourning

Book 8: Strength Enduring

Book 9: Forever Broken

Redwood Pack Series:

Book 1: An Alpha's Path

Book 2: A Taste for a Mate

Book 3: Trinity Bound

Redwood Pack Box Set (Contains Books 1-3)

Book 3.5: A Night Away

Book 4: Enforcer's Redemption

Book 4.5: Blurred Expectations

Book 4.7: Forgiveness

Book 5: Shattered Emotions

Book 6: Hidden Destiny

Book 6.5: A Beta's Haven

Book 7: Fighting Fate

Book 7.5: Loving the Omega

Book 7.7: The Hunted Heart

Book 8: Wicked Wolf

The Complete Redwood Pack Box Set (Contains Books

1-7.7)

The Branded Pack Series:
  (Written with Alexandra Ivy)
  Book 1: <u>Stolen and Forgiven</u>
  Book 2: Abandoned and Unseen
  Book 3: Buried and Shadowed

Dante's Circle Series:
  Book 1: Dust of My Wings
  Book 2: Her Warriors' Three Wishes
  Book 3: An Unlucky Moon
  The Dante's Circle Box Set (Contains Books 1-3)
  Book 3.5: His Choice
  Book 4: Tangled Innocence
  Book 5: Fierce Enchantment
  Book 6: An Immortal's Song
  Book 7: Prowled Darkness
  The Complete Dante's Circle Series (Contains Books 1-7)

Holiday, Montana Series:
  Book 1: Charmed Spirits
  Book 2: Santa's Executive
  Book 3: Finding Abigail
  The Holiday, Montana Box Set (Contains Books 1-3)
  Book 4: Her Lucky Love
  Book 5: Dreams of Ivory

The Complete Holiday, Montana Box Set (Contains Books 1-5)

The Happy Ever After Series:
Flame and Ink
Ink Ever After

Single Title:
Finally Found You

**Next From New York Times Bestselling Author Carrie
Ann Ryan's Whiskey and Lies**

Whiskey Secrets

Shocking pain slammed into his skull and down his back.
Dare Collins did his best not to scream in the middle of his
own bar. He slowly stood up and rubbed the back of his
head since he'd been distracted and hit it on the countertop.
Since the thing was made of solid wood and thick as hell, he
was surprised he hadn't given himself a concussion. But
since he didn't see double, he had a feeling once his long

night was over, he'd just have to make the throbbing go away with a glass of Macallan.

There was nothing better than a glass of smooth whiskey or an ice-cold mug of beer after a particularly long day. Which one Dare chose each night depended on not only his mood but also those around him. So was the life of a former cop turned bartender.

He had a feeling he'd be going for the whiskey and not a woman tonight—like most nights if he were honest. It had been a long day of inventory and no-show staff members. Meaning he had a headache from hell, and it looked as if he'd be working open to close when he truly didn't want to. But that's what happened when one was the owner of a bar and restaurant rather than just a manager or bartender— like he was with the Old Whiskey Restaurant and Bar.

It didn't help that his family had been in and out of the place all day for one reason or another—his brothers and parents either wanting something to eat or having a question that needed to be answered right away where a phone call or text wouldn't suffice. His mom and dad had mentioned more than once that he needed to be ready for their morning meeting, and he had a bad feeling in his gut about what that would mean for him later. But he pushed that from his thoughts because he was used to things in his life changing on a dime. He'd left the force for a reason, after all.

Enough of that.

He loved his family, he really did, but sometimes, they— his parents in particular—gave him a headache.

Since his mom and dad still ran the Old Whiskey Inn above his bar, they were constantly around, working their tails off at odd jobs that were far too hard for them at their ages, but they were all just trying to earn a living. When they weren't handling business for the inn, they were fixing problems upstairs that Dare wished they'd let him help with.

While he'd have preferred to call it a night and head back to his place a few blocks away, he knew that wouldn't happen tonight. Since his bartender, Rick, had called in sick at the last minute—as well as two of Dare's waitresses from the bar—Dare was pretty much screwed.

And if he wallowed just a little bit more, he might hear a tiny violin playing in his ear. He needed to get a grip and get over it. Working late and dealing with other people's mistakes was part of his job description, and he was usually fine with that.

Apparently, he was just a little off tonight. And since he knew himself well, he had a feeling it was because he was nearing the end of his time without his kid. Whenever he spent too many days away from Nathan, he acted like a crabby asshole. Thankfully, his weekend was coming up.

"Solving a hard math problem over there, or just daydreaming? Because that expression on your face looks like you're working your brain too hard. I'm surprised I don't see smoke coming out of your ears." Fox asked as he walked up to the bar, bringing Dare out of his thoughts. Dare had been pulling drafts and cleaning glasses mindlessly while in his head, but he was glad for the distraction, even if it annoyed him that he needed one.

Dare shook his head and flipped off his brother. "Suck me."

The bar was busy that night, so Fox sat down on one of the empty stools and grinned. "Nice way to greet your customers." He glanced over his shoulder before looking back at Dare and frowning. "Where are Rick and the rest of your staff?"

Dare barely held back a growl. "Out sick. Either there's really a twenty-four-hour stomach bug going around and I'm going to be screwed for the next couple of days, or they're all out on benders."

Fox cursed under his breath before hopping off his stool and going around the side of the large oak and maple bar to help out. That was Dare's family in a nutshell—they dropped everything whenever one of them needed help, and nobody even had to ask for it. Since Dare sucked at asking for help on a good day, he was glad that Fox knew what he needed without him having to say it.

Without asking, Fox pulled up a few drink orders and began mixing them with the skill of a long-time barkeep. Since Fox owned the small town newspaper—the Whiskey Chronicle—Dare was still surprised sometimes at how deft his younger brother was at working alongside him. Of course, even his parents, his older brother Loch, and his younger sister Tabby knew their way around the bar.

Just not as well as Dare did. Considering that this was *his* job, he was grateful for that.

He loved his family, his bar, and hell, he even loved his little town on the outskirts of Philly. Whiskey, Pennsylvania was like most other small towns in his state where some parts were new additions, and others were old stone buildings from the Revolutionary or Civil war eras with add-ons —like his.

And with a place called Whiskey, everyone attached the label where they could. Hence the town paper, his bar, and most of the other businesses around town. Only Loch's business really stood out with Loch's Security and Gym down the street, but that was just like Loch to be a little different yet still part of the town.

Whiskey had been named as such because of its old bootlegging days. It used to be called something else, but since Prohibition, the town had changed its name and cashed in on it. Whiskey was one of the last places in the country to keep Prohibition on the books, even with the nationwide decree. They'd fought to keep booze illegal, not for puritan reasons, but because their bootlegging market had helped the township thrive. Dare knew there was a lot more to it than that, but those were the stories the leaders told the tourists, and it helped with the flare.

Whiskey was located right on the Delaware River, so it overlooked New Jersey but was still on the Pennsylvania side of things. The main bridge that connected the two states through Whiskey and Ridge on the New Jersey side was one of the tourist spots for people to drive over and walk so they could be in two states at once while over the Delaware River.

Their town was steeped in history, and close enough to where George Washington had crossed the Delaware that they were able to gain revenue on the reenactments for the tourists, thus helping keep their town afloat.

The one main road through Whiskey that not only housed Loch's and Dare's businesses but also many of the other shops and restaurants in the area, was always jammed with cars and people looking for places to parallel park. Dare's personal parking lot for the bar and inn was a hot commodity.

And while he might like time to himself some days, he knew he wouldn't trade Whiskey's feel for any other place. They were a weird little town that was a mesh of history and newcomers, and he wouldn't trade it for the world. His sister Tabby might have moved out west and found her love and her place with the Montgomerys in Denver, but Dare knew he'd only ever find his home here.

Sure, he'd had a few flings in Denver when he visited his sister, but he knew they'd never be more than one night or two. Hell, he was the king of flings these days, and that was for good reason. He didn't need commitment or attachments beyond his family and his son, Nathan.

Time with Nathan's mom had proven that to him, after all.

"You're still daydreaming over there," Fox called out from the other side of the bar. "You okay?"

Dare nodded, frowning. "Yeah, I think I need more caffeine or something since my mind keeps wandering." He pasted on his trademark grin and went to help one of the new arrivals who'd taken a seat at the bar. Dare wasn't the broody one of the family—that honor went to Loch—and he hated when he acted like it.

"What can I get you?" he asked a young couple that had taken two empty seats at the bar. They had matching wedding bands on their fingers but looked to be in their early twenties.

He couldn't imagine being married that young. Hell, he'd never been married, and he was in his mid-thirties now. He hadn't married Monica even though she'd given him Nathan, and even now, he wasn't sure they'd have ever taken that step even if they had stayed together. She had Auggie now, and he had...well, he had his bar.

That wasn't depressing at all.

"Two Yuenglings please, draft if you have it," the guy said, smiling.

Dare nodded. "Gonna need to see your IDs, but I do have it on tap for you." As Yuengling was a Pennsylvania beer, not having it outside the bottle would be stupid even in a town that prided itself on whiskey.

The couple pulled out their IDs, and Dare checked them quickly. Since both were now the ripe age of twenty-two, he went to pull them their beers and set out their check since they weren't looking to run a tab.

Another woman with long, caramel brown hair with hints of red came to sit at the edge of the bar. Her hair lay in loose waves down her back and she had on a sexy-as-fuck green dress that draped over her body to showcase sexy curves and legs that seemed to go on forever. The garment didn't have sleeves so he could see the toned muscles in her arms work as she picked up a menu to look at it. When she looked up, she gave him a dismissive glance before focusing on the menu again. He held back a sigh. Not in the mood to deal with whatever that was about, he let Fox take care of her and put her from his mind. No use dealing with a woman who clearly didn't want him near, even if it were just to take a drink order. Funny, he usually had to speak to a female before making her want him out of the picture. At least, that's what he'd learned from Monica.

And why the hell was he thinking about his ex again? He usually only thought of her in passing when he was talking to Nathan or hanging out with his kid for the one weekend a month the custody agreement let Dare have him. Having been in a dangerous job and then becoming a bartender didn't look good to some lawyers it seemed, at least when Monica had fought for full custody after Nathan was born.

He pushed those thoughts from his mind, however, not in the mood to scare anyone with a scowl on his face by remembering how his ex had looked down on him for his occupation even though she'd been happy to slum it with him when it came to getting her rocks off.

Dare went through the motions of mixing a few more drinks before leaving Fox to tend to the bar so he could go check on the restaurant part of the building.

Since the place had originally been an old stone inn on both floors instead of just the top one, it was set up a little differently than most newer buildings around town. The bar was off to one side; the restaurant area where they served delicious, higher-end entrees and tapas was on the other. Most people needed a reservation to sit down and eat in the main restaurant area, but the bar also had seating for dinner, only their menu wasn't quite as extensive and ran closer to bar food.

In the past, he'd never imagined he would be running something like this, even though his parents had run a smaller version of it when he was a kid. But none of his siblings had been interested in taking over once his parents wanted to retire from the bar part and only run the inn. When Dare decided to leave the force only a few years in, he'd found his place here, however reluctantly.

Being a cop hadn't been for him, just like being in a relationship. He'd thought he would be able to do the former, but life had taken a turn, and he'd faced his mortality far sooner than he bargained for. Apparently, being a gruff, perpetually single bar owner was more his speed, and he was pretty damn good at it, too. Most days, anyway.

His house manager over on the restaurant side was running from one thing to another, but from the outside, no one would have noticed. Claire was just that good. She was in her early fifties and already a grandmother, but she didn't look a day over thirty-five with her smooth, dark skin and bright smile. Good genes and makeup did wonders— according to her anyway. He'd be damned if he'd say that. His mother and Tabby had taught him *something* over the years.

The restaurant was short-staffed but managing, and he was grateful he had Claire working long hours like he did.

He oversaw it all, but he knew he couldn't have done it without her. After making sure she didn't need anything, he headed back to the bar to relieve Fox. The rush was finally dying down now, and his brother could just sit back and enjoy a beer since Dare knew he'd already worked a long day at the paper.

By the time the restaurant closed and the bar only held a few dwindling costumers, Dare was ready to go to bed and forget the whole lagging day. Of course, he still had to close out the two businesses and talk to both Fox and Loch since his older brother had shown up a few moments ago. Maybe he'd get them to help him close out so he wouldn't be here until midnight. He must be tired if the thought of closing out was too much for him.

"So, Rick didn't show, huh?" Loch asked as he stood up from his stool. His older brother started cleaning up beside Fox, and Dare held back a smile. He'd have to repay them in something other than beer, but he knew they were working alongside him because they were family and had the time; they weren't doing it for rewards.

"Nope. Shelly and Kayla didn't show up either." Dare resisted the urge to grind his teeth at that. "Thanks for help-ing. I'm exhausted and wasn't in the mood to deal with this all alone."

"That's what we're here for," Loch said with a shrug.

"By the way, you have any idea what this seven a.m. meeting tomorrow is about?" Fox asked after a moment. "They're putting Tabby on speaker phone for it and everything."

Dare let out a sigh. "I'm not in the mood to deal with any meeting that early. I have no idea what it's going to be about, but I have a bad feeling."

"Seems like they have an announcement." Loch sat back down on his stool and scrolled through his phone. He was constantly working or checking on his daughter, so his phone was strapped to him at all times. Misty had to be with Loch's best friend, Ainsley, since his brother worked that night. Ainsley helped out when Loch needed a night to work or see Dare. Loch had full custody of Misty, and being a single father wasn't easy.

Dare had a feeling no matter what his parents had to say, things were going to be rocky after the morning meeting. His parents were caring, helpful, and always wanted the best for their family. That also meant they tended to be slightly overbearing in the most loving way possible.

"Well, shit."

It looked like he'd go without whiskey *or* a woman tonight.

Of course, an image of the woman with gorgeous hair and that look of disdain filled his mind, and he held back a sigh. Once again, Dare was a glutton for punishment, even in his thoughts.

The next morning, he cupped his mug of coffee in his hands and prayed his eyes would stay open. He'd stupidly gotten caught up on paperwork the night before and was now running on about three hours of sleep.

Loch sat in one of the booths with Misty, watching as

she colored in her coloring book. She was the same age as Nathan, which Dare always appreciated since the cousins could grow up like siblings—on weekends when Dare had Nathan that was. The two kids got along great, and he hoped that continued throughout the cootie phases kids seemed to get sporadically.

Fox sat next to Dare at one of the tables with his laptop open. Since his brother owned the town paper, he was always up-to-date on current events and was even now typing up something.

They had Dare's phone between them with Tabby on the other line, though she wasn't saying anything. Her fiancé, Alex, was probably near as well since those two seemed to be attached at the hip. Considering his future brother-in-law adored Tabby, Dare didn't mind that as much as he probably should have as a big brother.

The elder Collinses stood at the bar, smiles on their faces, yet Dare saw nervousness in their stances. He'd been a cop too long to miss it. They were up to something, and he had a feeling he wasn't going to like it.

"Just get it over with," Dare said, keeping his language decent—not only for Misty but also because his mother would still take him by the ear if he cursed in front of her.

But because his tone had bordered on rude, his mother still raised a brow, and he sighed. Yep, he had a really bad feeling about this.

"Good morning to you, too, Dare," Bob Collins said with a snort and shook his head. "Well, since you're all here, even our baby girl, Tabby—"

"Not a baby, Dad!" Tabby called out from the phone, and the rest of them laughed, breaking the tension slightly.

"Yeah, we're not babies," Misty put in, causing everyone to laugh even harder.

"Anyway," Barbara Collins said with a twinkle in her eye. "We have an announcement to make." She rolled her shoulders back, and Dare narrowed his eyes. "As you know, your father and I have been nearing the age of retirement for a while now, but we still wanted to run our inn as innkeepers rather that merely owners."

"Finally taking a vacation?" Dare asked. His parents worked far too hard and wouldn't let their kids help them. He'd done what he could by buying the bar from them when he retired from the force and then built the restaurant himself.

"If you'd let me finish, young man, I'd let you know," his mother said coolly, though there was still warmth in her eyes. That was his mother in a nutshell. She'd reprimand, but soothe the sting, too.

"Sorry," he mumbled, and Fox coughed to cover up a laugh. If Dare looked behind him, he figured he'd see Loch hiding a smile of his own.

Tabby laughed outright.

Damn little sisters.

"So, as I was saying, we've worked hard. But, lately, it seems like we've worked *too* hard." She looked over at his dad and smiled softly, taking her husband's hand. "It's time to make some changes around here."

Dare sat up straighter.

"We're retiring. Somewhat. The inn hasn't been doing as well as it did back when it was with your grandparents, and part of that is on the economy. But part of that is on us. What we want to do is renovate more and update the existing rooms and service. In order to do that and step back as innkeepers, we've hired a new person."

"You're kidding me, right?" Dare asked, frowning. "You can't just hire someone to take over and work in our building without even talking to us. And it's not like I have time to help her run it when she doesn't know how you like things."

"You won't be running it," Bob said calmly. "Not yet, anyway. Your mom and I haven't fully retired, and you know it. We've been running the inn for years, but now we want to step away. Something *you've* told us we should do. So, we hired someone. One who knows how to handle this kind of transition and will work with the construction crew and us. She has a lot of experience from working in Philly and New York and will be an asset."

Dare fisted his hands by his sides and blew out a breath. They had to be fucking kidding. "It sounds like you've done your research and already made your decision. Without asking us. Without asking *me*."

His mother gave him a sad look. "We've always wanted to do this, Dare, you know that."

"Yes. But you should have talked to us. And renovating like this? I didn't know you wanted to. We could have helped." He didn't know why he was so angry, but being kept out of the loop was probably most of it.

His father signed. "We've been looking into this for years, even before you came back to Whiskey and bought the bar from us. And while it may seem like this is out of the blue, we've been doing the research for a while. Yes, we should have told you, but everything came up all at once recently, and we wanted to show you the plans when we had details rather than get your hopes up and end up not doing it."

Dare just blinked. There was so much in that statement —in *all* of those statements—that he couldn't quite process it. And though he could have yelled about any of it just then, his mind fixed on the one thing that annoyed him the most.

"So, you're going to have some city girl come into *my* place and order me around? I don't think so."

"And why not? Have a problem with listening to women?"

Dare stiffened because that last part hadn't come from his family. No. He turned toward the voice. It had come from the woman he'd seen the night before in the green dress.

And because fate liked to fuck with him, he had a feeling he knew *exactly* who this person was.

Their newly hired innkeeper.

And new thorn in his side.

Find out more in Whiskey Secrets.
To make sure you're up to date on all of Carrie Ann's releases, sign up for her mailing list HERE.

DELICATE INK

From New York Times Bestselling Author Carrie Ann
Ryan's Montgomery Ink Series

DELICATE INK

On the wrong side of thirty, Austin Montgomery is ready to settle down. Unfortunately, his inked sleeves and scruffy beard isn't the suave business appearance some women crave. Only finding a woman who can deal with his job, as a tattoo artist and owner of Montgomery Ink, his seven meddling siblings, and his own gruff attitude won't be easy.

Finding a man is the last thing on Sierra Elder's mind. A recent transplant to Denver, her focus is on opening her own boutique. Wanting to cover up scars that run deeper than her flesh, she finds in Austin a man that truly gets to her—in more ways than one.

Although wary, they embark on a slow, tempestuous burn of a relationship. When blasts from both their pasts intrude on their present, however, it will take more than a promise of what could be to keep them together.

Find out more in DELICATE INK
To make sure you're up to date on all of Carrie Ann's releases, sign up for her mailing list HERE.

LOVE RESTORED

From New York Times Bestselling Author Carrie Ann Ryan's Gallagher Brothers series

In the first of a Montgomery Ink spin-off series from NYT Bestselling Author Carrie Ann Ryan, a broken man uncovers the truth of what it means to take a second chance with the most unexpected woman...

Graham Gallagher has seen it all. And when tragedy struck, lost it all. He's been the backbone of his brothers, the one they all rely on in their lives and business. And when it comes to falling in love and creating a life, he knows what it's like to have it all and watch it crumble. He's done with looking for another person to warm his bed, but apparently he didn't learn his lesson because the new piercer at Montgomery Ink tempts him like no other.

Blake Brennen may have been born a trust fund baby, but she's created a whole new life for herself in the world of ink, piercings, and freedom. Only the ties she'd thought she'd cut long ago aren't as severed as she'd believed. When she finds Graham constantly in her path, she knows from first glance that he's the wrong kind of guy for her. Except that Blake excels at making the wrong choice and Graham might be the ultimate temptation for the bad girl she'd thought long buried.

Find out more in Love Restored

To make sure you're up to date on all of Carrie Ann's releases, sign up for her mailing list HERE.